STORIES FROM THE ATTIC

C C Writers

Copyright © 2022 Collierville Christian Writers

All rights reserved. No part of this book may be reproduced without the express written consent of the publisher and the authors except in the case of brief quotations as part of articles and reviews.

The events and characters described in each work of fiction in this anthology are imaginary and are not intended to refer to specific places or persons. The work of each author represented in this anthology, whether fiction or nonfiction, belongs solely to that author and does not represent the opinions or thoughts of the publisher, editors, leadership or other members of the Collierville Christian Writers Group.

ABOUT THIS BOOK

These original short stories were written by members of Collierville Christian Writers, based in Collierville, Tennessee. Inspired by the single premise of a "story from the attic", this diverse collection reflects the creativity and opinion of each writer.

We hope you enjoy this collaboration and that it inspires you to pursue the treasures that await you in unexpected places.

Special thanks:
Annette Cole Mastron, Editor
Gary Fearon, Creative Director
Barbara Ragsdale and Jan Wertz, proofreaders

CONTENTS

STORIES FROM THE ATTIC

Don't know what I might find —
    tales from the attic —
treasures of every kind

Against the angled roof, I wind
    just below the stain from an old water leak —
don't know what I might find

There are mementos of different size, lined
    atop rusty metal and musty wood antique
treasures of every kind

A huge trunk, filled with memories, enshrined —
    lifting the lid, into the crate I peek;
don't know what I might find

Old toys, clothes, and knickknacks are beside
    cherished letters, photographs, and jewelry — aesthetic
treasures of every kind

Many a thing have a secret and meaning, sublime —
each with a story and mystery, unique;
don't know what I might find
treasures of every kind

John Burgette

THE CLUTTER BUSTERS

Kay DiBianca

"What a mess!" I stood in the middle of the disorganized jumble of boxes and old furniture, otherwise known as my attic, and shook my head. A million tiny dust particles floated in the column of sunlight radiating through the attic window.

I had spent all morning inventing excuses for why I shouldn't clean out the clutter that had accumulated over the last five years, but even I have a limit to procrastination. "Rebecca," I said out loud to myself. "You need to get to work."

I decided the first thing I should do was take a break and organize my thoughts. You know, put together a plan. I moved a box off of an old recliner I meant to donate to Goodwill a few years ago, and I sat down.

I had forgotten how comfortable that old chair was. I leaned back and lolled against the soft headrest. My eyes felt heavy, and I fell into a deep sleep.

I dreamed I was in a dark cavern with thick dust swirling all around me. When I tried to brush it away, the dust tickled my nose. "Ah … ah … ah …" I couldn't stop it. "AHCHOO!" It was a monstrous sneeze, loud enough to register on the Richter scale. My head ricocheted back against the chair, and the whole house shook.

"AARGH!" I heard a tiny voice, much higher-pitched than mine. "What a noise!"

I jerked upright in the chair. "Who's there?" I demanded, looking right and left and trying to sound like I was in command, even though my heart was beating like a crazed bongo drummer. "Who's in my house?" I shouted.

A sparkling streak of glitter whooshed out from behind an old, discarded bookcase. Marching out right behind the silvery mist was a little man. He was about six inches tall, and he was wearing a suit and tie. He had a red beret on his head, and he pointed at me with a long, gnarly finger. "That was a terrible commotion. You scared me half to death."

Now I'm not the world's smartest person, but I know there's no such thing as faeries or whatever you call them. "I must be dreaming," I said out loud and rubbed my eyes.

The little man jammed his hands on his hips and peered at me with an expression of utter disdain on his face. "That's what they all say, sister. Humans try to pretend we don't exist until we show up and scare the heck out of them."

I felt my mouth hanging open. "Who are you?"

"I'm Bernie." He thumbed a gesture toward the bookcase. "Viola and Steve are hiding behind your furniture."

Sure enough, as soon as he spoke, two more little people waltzed out. One was a plump and pleasant looking lady holding a star-tipped wand and wearing a gold crown on her head. The other was a youngish-looking boy. The kid tripped over the bottom of a floor lamp and did a face plant right in front of me.

"Steve, are you all right?" the lady faerie asked.

"Yes ma'am," the little guy said. He stood and she helped him brush off his clothes. With every stroke of her hand, a wisp of gold faerie dust materialized.

If this was a dream, it was my dream, so I decided to make the most of it. "Who are you?" I demanded. "And what are you doing in my attic?"

The nice lady faerie waved her wand and more gold particles streaked across the room. "We're so sorry if we frightened you, but your sneeze woke us up." She patted her hair in place. "Let me introduce ourselves. You've already met Bernie." She nodded toward the little man leaning back against a cardboard box with his hands behind his head and one leg crossed over the other knee. Then she pointed to the little clumsy one. "This is Steve, and I'm Viola. We're the Clutter Busters."

"The what?"

"The Clutter Busters," she said again.

The young one, Steve, piped up. "We help people clean the

clutter out of their lives."

I looked around the attic. It was still a disorganized mess. "Well, it doesn't look like you've done much for me," I retorted. Sarcasm is one of my talents.

"Watch it, sister." Bernie jumped up and stood on one of the boxes.

"Now, Bernie, don't be so impatient," Viola said.

"Well, she's one of those humans who thinks she knows it all. Uppity type." Bernie crossed his tiny arms over his chest and paced back and forth on top of the box.

Viola turned back to me. "Our job isn't to do the work *for* you. We are here to *help* you unclutter your life."

"You're going to help me with all this clutter?" I waved my arm around the attic.

"Not that clutter, yo-yo." Bernie jumped up on the arm of my chair. "The clutter in there." He tapped on the side of my head with his little fist.

"Hey! Stop that," I shouted and tried to push him away, but he floated up to the top of a stack of boxes and looked down at me with a big smirk on his face.

"Now, Bernie," Viola said. "Don't be rude. We need to work with Rebecca."

"How do you know my name?"

"We know everything about you, sister," Bernie said. "We've been up here for the past month."

"You've been living in my attic for a month? And spying on me?"

"Not exactly spying, dear," Viola said. "We've been getting to know you."

Now I was mad. These people - er, faeries - moved into my home without even a "How dee doo," and set up housekeeping in my attic. "And how exactly did you plan on getting to know me by living in my attic?" I demanded.

"We read your diary," Bernie said with a big grin on his face.

"You WHAT?" I shrieked and tried to stand up, but my arms were weighed down to the chair and I couldn't move. Bernie sat on one of them and Steve on the other. Those little guys weighed a ton.

"I'm very sorry, Rebecca," Viola said with an apologetic tilt of her head, "but it was the best way for us to know who you are and how we can help you."

"I'm just fine, thank you. I don't need any help from … whatever you are."

"We're faeries," Steve said and blushed. "I'm just an apprentice, but I'm earning my bronze faerie dust on this project."

"I don't care who or what you are. I don't need any help with my life, and I want you to leave." I pointed to the stairs.

"Actually, Rebecca, you do need help." Viola said in her sweet little voice as she flew up onto the desk next to my chair. "Your diary reveals that you've developed some negative personality traits. Things like jealousy and bitterness."

"Me? Jealous and bitter. You must be kidding. That doesn't describe me at all."

"Oh yeah?" Bernie hopped down and stood next to my diary that was lying on the old desk. He made a great show of opening it and turning some of the pages that were almost as big as he was.

"How about this little gem," he said and read aloud from my diary. "Pamela is such a flirt. Her stiletto heels make a little tap-tap melody on the linoleum floor when she sashays to the coffee room, her too-short, too-tight mini-skirt clinging to her swaying hips. She makes me sick." He looked up and took off his miniature glasses. "Sounds like a little green-eyed envy to me."

"I am not jealous of Pamela. I'm just being honest. She's a flirt."

"We noticed you wear mini-skirts, and you always go to the coffee room when Brandon is there," Steve said.

"You spied on me at work?" I was beginning to wonder if I could sue faeries.

"It's not really spying, dear," Viola said. "We're just observing your behavior."

I shook my head in disbelief.

Bernie turned a couple of more pages in the diary. "How about this description of Jim?" He cleared his throat and pointed to an entry I made a month ago. "They gave the promotion to Jim. Just because he's the boss's son-in-law, he got preference. I should quit." Bernie peered at me over his glasses. "Sounds like bitterness to me, Tootsie. You just can't say anything nice about any of your coworkers."

"That's not true! I like the people I work with and they like me," I said, but I felt a nagging sense of guilt tugging at me.

Bernie picked up the red book and flung it in my lap. "Here ya go. Find one place where you said something nice about someone else."

I felt the heat rising in my face as I flipped through the pages. All I saw were complaints about other people. I couldn't believe I had written this junk. I let the book drop into my lap and hung my head in shame. "I never realized I was such a small person," I said.

"Hey. Watch what you say about small people," Bernie said, and for the first time he laughed and elbowed Steve.

I looked to Viola for help.

She flew up onto the arm of my chair and put her delicate little hand on my shoulder. "You've taken the first step, Rebecca," she said. "You've admitted that you've been wrong. Most people don't realize that thoughts turn into words and words not only hurt the people they're directed against, but they hurt the person who's thinking and saying them." She patted my shoulder.

"What can I do?" I asked.

"We noticed that you're an excellent writer. Why don't you try writing a novel?" Viola said, and gold dust shimmered around her head. "You can write stories about some of the characters in your diary, but you can imagine them in different ways. Maybe Pamela could be the heroine of a book. Writing is a creative way to clean up all the mental and emotional clutter we carry around, and along the way you'll probably learn a lot about yourself."

"I've always wanted to write," I said, "but I'm not sure I have the talent for it."

"Remember what Walt Disney said. 'All our dreams can come

true if we have the courage to pursue them.'" Viola smiled softly. "You can do this, Rebecca."

"Thank you, Viola," I said. "I hope you three can stay with me for a while."

"Oh, no, dear. Our work here is done, and we have other jobs. I think we're scheduled to pay a visit to Pamela next." She turned and pointed her wand at me. My chin dropped to my chest and I fell asleep.

ঌ

When I woke up, the attic was bathed in a soft light. *It must be late afternoon*, I thought. I looked up at the window, expecting to see a splash of gold and silver glitter, but it was just the same old dust that was there before. There was no change in the disorganized mess. *What a strange dream!*

I stood and yawned. How funny that I learned something important in a ridiculous dream about faeries. I walked to the desk and picked up my red diary. When I opened it, all the pages had been torn out. Only the cover of the book was left.

I stood there trying to understand when I noticed a dark blue book lying on the back of the desk. The cover said *Rebecca's First Novel.* I opened it with trembling hands. Inside, all the pages were blank except for the first one. It said, "Good luck, Rebecca!" Beneath it were three tiny handprints, one gold, one silver, and one bronze.

THE DONATION

Beth Krewson Carter

The cool air hits me as soon as I open the door. I file in behind the dinner crowd and stand against the wall where I'm finally shielded from the blood orange sunset baking the parking lot. When it's my turn, I step up to the hostess stand and nod to the manager. After a week of patronage and good tips, he simply smiles at me when I slip alone into the restaurant's bar.

Bottles clink above the murmured voices as I make my way towards a lone stool. The bartender, whose name I've learned is Stan, is wiping glasses at the end of the bar. He likes to flirt and I'm always a sucker for his weak jokes. On another evening, he might have made his way towards me, but he glances up at my red rimmed eyes and keeps his distance. Much like my job at the hospital, his line of work has taught him to read faces and skip the jovial comments when pain is evident.

Without a word, I watch Stan's expert hands pour and swirl his creations. He makes me my usual drink, a vodka tonic that looks like water when he's done, but I shake my head and motion for a soda. After the day I've had, the last thing I need is another depressant.

"Thanks," I say when the tumbler lands on my napkin.

"Hard day?" Stan asks.

I nod, feeling his eyes study me while I sip and I'm grateful for his silent understanding. After a long moment, he steps away, leaving me in peace. Out of the corner of my eye, I watch him start to serve another customer. He reads their body language with precision, and I'm reminded of why I like him. Stan is a master of all things human.

For a moment, I consider calling him over, to seek out his wise counsel, but the envelope in the pocket of my jeans stops me. I know my whole story is far too complicated for a casual exchange. Maybe I'm just afraid that Stan might listen. Then he would ask me why I wasn't more wary of the old man, and I know I won't have an answer for that one.

The truth is that my only real motivation was to help Mama. I guess that's the problem with being an only child. You take on adult roles and volunteer for tasks, especially when the one person who raised you is battling cancer.

Of course, cleaning out an attic seemed like the least I could do for her. Besides, I knew Mama really didn't want to set foot in that house. She always told me that she left home at an early age, and that the old midtown bungalow still makes her skin crawl. We only ever went over there on Christmas Eve and Father's Day, and even then, she was on edge.

By the time I was twelve, my mouth did most of the talking during our brief visits. Mama and I would sit side by side on the heavy furniture in the formal living room, and I would ramble on about anything, just so we could leave as early as possible. There was always a sense of relief for both of us when our car would finally pull away from the curb. I would turn around to watch the white columns on the front of the house grow smaller and smaller, and after a few miles, our anxiety would start to fade. Then Mama would make me laugh by telling me how eager she was to drown out our memories of that place with a pitcher of sweet tea and pile of smoked barbeque.

Gramps, that's what I called him, lived in the sprawling house and I always knew he had a hard way of looking at life. When I was younger, I assumed that meant he was strict. The authoritative way he carried himself coupled with his stern shoulders and giant forearms was slightly frightening. He worked as a cotton merchant, which was interesting, except that he always had a look in his eye whenever he talked about his business deals. During those conversations, his gaze felt like steel, making me glad I never had to negotiate with him.

"I'll clean out the attic and give you a break," I told Mama last week when I brought dinner over to her house.

"Would you?" she asked, pushing her Pad Thai around on her plate, hoping I wouldn't notice her poor appetite.

"No problem. I have the whole week off from the hospital. I don't think there's much left, and a couple of days should do it. Besides, I love the restaurants in Midtown. You can schedule the estate sale and cleaning crew when I'm done."

She simply nodded, then reached over to take my hand. Her boney fingers felt cold on my skin, and I hoped that my offer of a few days of labor would nudge her to keep fighting.

I twirl the ice in my glass and for the first time, I wonder if Mama knew who her father really was. Maybe she understood, better than I did, the type of beliefs he held. All afternoon, I've been thinking about questions like that. There's so much I need to ask her and I long to hear her voice. It might be childish, but carrying this secret around feels like it might break me tonight.

My fingers start to fumble with my phone until I look down at my screen saver. I stare at the image and for a minute, it's like I could reach back through time and touch her. The picture was taken at my graduation from nursing school. Mama looks so happy with her hair brushing her collar bone and her soft, round figure. I swallow hard because the mother I have now wears a scarf and is brittle. That's when I put the phone face down on the bar. There's no use in adding more hurt to someone you love when they've already had enough heartache in life to fill the Mississippi River.

The phone goes back in my pocket but not before my hand grazes the bulky envelope. On instinct, my fingers draw back, because any gift can be diminished by the truth.

"This is for you," my mother told me earlier in the day when I stopped by to see her.

She pressed the yellowed envelope in my hand. The weight of all the paper told me there was money right inside the flap, but I hesitated. Cancer treatments are expensive when your health insurance has stopped paying, and all of Mama's inheritance was finally going to stop the bill collectors from harassing her.

"He wanted you to have what was in his safe. It's not much, because of his gambling, but you said you wanted a new car, and this should help."

I remember smiling at that moment. As a first-year employee, all I've been able to afford up to this point are my student loan payments and rent. My car runs well enough, but Mama knows how I've longed for more than basic transportation. Getting to the hospital for the night shift would be so much nicer if I had reliable heat in the winter and air conditioning that didn't sometimes involve rolling down four windows and driving sixty mile an hour. If only I hadn't looked behind the water heater, then I could be planning a trip to the dealership for a test drive.

The problem was that the lone trunk looked so odd, just sitting there in the corner. When I first saw the dusty box, my only thought was to simply add it to all the other old furniture I was piling together on the floor. My back was aching, so I grabbed the antique chest without much thought. I almost left the lid shut, almost, but I didn't, because the top reminded me of a pirate's treasure.

Old locks always make me curious, so I stopped to look at the one I was holding. The latch was shiny; the way old metal never is, so I tried the clasp. To my surprise, the mechanism opened with ease. Was it worn from constant use? I've thought about that for hours, especially after what I found.

At first, I thought they were just a bunch of old sheets. I was just about to pitch them into the trash when something caught my eye. A small point in the muslin seemed out of place. I grabbed the simple white cotton and stared in horror as a Klansman's hood unfolded.

My hands were trembling like an earthquake, but I managed to rip up the fabric in a matter of minutes. I threw the long strips in the dumpster outside, and then I buried the cloth under all the rest of the junk from the attic. By the time I was finished, every reminder of Gramps, except for the heavy furniture, was gone from that house.

I shake my head because now the money in my pocket starts to feel like a curse. Staring into my glass, I wonder what I should do. I rub my temples until I remember another hopeless situation.

It was last winter, and a young gunshot victim was rushed into the emergency room. He was thirteen years old, with the thinnest arms I've ever seen. His wounds were severe, so I started a central line and helped the young intern on call to stabilize him. We worked at a frantic pace until they took the patient up for surgery. That's when the doctor and I finally stopped. There was blood on the floor and the area was a wreck. At that moment, we looked at each and thought the same thing. Does the hate and violence ever stop?

I place a few dollars under my glass, and Stan catches my eye. He merely nods, letting me know that I have a raincheck on his charm. When I go outside, the sunset has faded into a navy velvet night. I ignore the exhaust fumes lingering over the parking lot and start my engine. Poplar Avenue stretches out like a long ribbon, and I travel east until I reach the small community where Mama and I used to bring the mobile food pantry.

Despite the total darkness, I manage to find the right place. For years, part of Mama's job involved feeding rural families. Sometimes I rode with her, and we always came to this exact single-story building.

My tires crunch on the gravel, and a soft glow from the windows spills over the handful of cars that are lined up against the wall. I pull around to the side entrance, and I smile when I see that the signs for the youth center and clothes closet are still there.

I haven't been in church in years, but I step inside the office door and hope for the best. Music, played on a piano, floats through the air. I start to walk towards the Gospel hymns, assuming choir practice is starting, but a voice at my back startles me.

"May I help you?"

I turn to find an older man in a slightly frayed suit. He has a Bible in one hand and some papers in the other. His face is the color of rich mahogany and I recognize him as the minister. He holds my gaze but from his expression, I can tell that he doesn't remember me.

For a minute, I don't speak because I'm not sure where to begin. I stand there and wonder what he must think of me. Maybe I just look like a white girl in sweat-stained clothes, with her hair in a ponytail. Maybe he sees me or maybe he doesn't, but I bet he knows my soul needs salvation.

"I hope so," I finally say, "you see, I need to make a donation."

SECRET POCKET

Barbara Ragsdale

"Attic? What attic?" I stared at my mother in disbelief. "We've been here a week gutting the family home so it can be sold, and I've never heard anything about an attic."

"Now, Kimberley, don't get all hot and bothered. It's just a small space over the kitchen. Shouldn't be much up there."

"How come I don't know where it is?"

"Because it's hidden. The stairs are behind one of the cabinets. Come, I'll show you. It's been years since I've been up there."

Mom marched over to a tall cabinet, its shelves once filled with staples. Empty now because we'd thrown everything away. I rubbed my hand over the metal shelf under the built-in flour sifter. Remnants of white powder remained in the seams from the hundreds of rolled dough for pie crusts and buttermilk biscuits.

Mom peered behind the cabinet to reach for a small lever. Suddenly, the wall moved to reveal hidden stairs. My imagination went into overdrive conjuring up all manner of reasons why a hidden wall was needed.

"Did they hide liquor up here?" I asked, remembering Prohibition.

"No, silly. The old still was hidden in the trees, close to the stream, but never discovered by the revenuers." She giggled the whole time giving me the skinny on my great-grandparents' illegal activities.

"Are you kidding me?"

"Just a little. I was told it wasn't much of an operation and didn't last long. Grandmother Rachel marched with the Women's Christian Temperance Union. She couldn't have home brew in the house. However, she did like her evening hot toddy," both of us laughing at the absurd situation.

I started up the stairs feeling my way along the wall for a light switch. "Is there a switch or string to pull for some light? I didn't bring candles."

Mom grunted and marched ahead of me up the stairs, the flashlight on her cell phone leading the way. I heard her gasp at the top. The room was crammed full. The ceiling so low we couldn't stand up straight. No windows and sharp gables surrounded the space. What a nightmare.

"I don't believe it. Not much up here, you said. Uncle Dirk must have stood at the top of the stairs and just thrown the stuff anywhere."

"I doubt my brother ever set foot in this place. More likely he made Annie do it." The maid had served the family for years. After Dirk's death Annie retired for much needed rest. Mom and I treat her to lunch once a week.

In the dim light from an overhead bulb, I tiptoed a path through the boxes. "We're going to have to open every one of these." My back hurt and my knees argued about stooping and bending. "If there are any critters in these boxes, I'm running and screaming."

"I'll be right behind you, but I doubt there are any." Mom could sometimes be the bright light of enthusiasm or a total fibber. I found a box that wasn't taped closed, sneezed from the dust and pulled on the cardboard. I opened it up wide to let out any unwanted visitors. Nothing happened. I flashed a light from my cell on the contents. "These are bank records. Account ledgers." The family had been the only savings and loan institution in the city for many years.

"What are the dates?" she asked.

"The 1940s. We either shred or burn them. Some of these people are still living." Our task just got bigger. I moved the box aside to grab one that was taped closed. Inside were diaries. "Did grandmother keep journals?"

"Oh, yes. All the time. She wrote what happened every day, including the weather."

"Well, I've found them. She must have known everybody in town because she names them all," I said, flipping through the many pages. "These are fascinating. She never learned to drive, did she?"

"Nope, and never had a car. If she wanted anything she walked. Put on her red hat and away she'd go."

"Okay, let's start hauling boxes down because it's too hot up here and I can't stand up. You slide them down the steps while I catch them at the bottom." For the next hour Mom dragged and shoved the boxes down and I stacked them in the kitchen dreading the final job—disposing of the contents.

I made a trip up the stairs to see how much was left. My eyes spied a form in a far corner. "What's that?" Mom looked surprised.

"Oh, that's Grandmother Rachel's dress form. She had all her dresses handmade." I stepped through the remaining boxes to stand in front of the covered form.

"Is this one of her dresses?" looking at a beautiful full lace gown, long sleeves and sweetheart neckline draped on the form. "Looks like a wedding dress to me. Was her waist that small?" My ribs hurt at the thought of being wrapped so tight and envious if she was that tiny.

"It is a wedding gown," Mom confirmed. "And I remember a tale I thought was pure fiction about her having a wedding dress that had a secret pocket. For what, I don't know. But this dress isn't the one she wore to marry Grandfather Logan." Mom twisted the form around to the back and began to take the gown off by slipping it up over the top. She turned it inside out and ran her hand around the waist band. "Yes, here it is." She pulled out a piece of folded paper from the small pocket and began to read.

"What's that?" I asked, bothered by the strange expression on her face, the kind of expression where you just learned something you wished you hadn't. Hesitating, she handed me the tattered square. I read aloud.

"Oh, willow, sweet willow, weep for me.
My love waits beside the tree.
A promise I cannot keep; a grief I cannot share.
Forgive me, Dru, for not being there."

"Who's Dru? Is this for real or a poem?" My mind raced full of questions.

"I'm not sure, but I'm afraid it isn't just a poem." She uncurled her hand. A used railroad ticket stub rested there. "It's for St. Louis. There were rumors, whispers really, that grandmother wanted to marry someone else and couldn't."

"Maybe it's in the journals," I said, very excited ready to dig into the family history even if it might be scandal ridden. "I love juicy stories."

"Be careful what you ask for," Mom chided as the rest of the boxes tumbled down the stairs. I wrestled the dressmaking form from the attic and stood to eye the reminder of a time past.

"That's it," I said sizing up the next steps. "You take these boxes. I'll get the rest and the dressmaker form is going to Natalie's daughter who sews all the time."

"Where are the journals?" she muttered while loading her boxes on the trolley I'd remembered to bring. She groaned, stretching her back. "I need a massage," rubbing her tired muscles.

"I've got them. Don't have time for a massage, but I can read while I take a hot bath," laughing through the fatigue. We loaded both cars and started for home. "Burn the ledgers. There're too many to shred," I added.

"I've still got the burn pit I used for the leaves last fall. Don't worry, I'll check dates. Dirk didn't like the bank and only went when he needed money."

She waved a kiss and drove the car toward home. The day had been long, and I was exhausted. I took one final look at the empty house that held such pleasant memories for me until Uncle Dirk inherited it after grandfather's death. He was always asking Mom for money. If gossip was true, she wasn't the only woman he tried to charm for financial support. Didn't work on Mom.

Dru, who are you? Family secrets. The unknown held more interest for me that trying to find out who Uncle Dirk swindled. I skipped reading the books that evening. Too tired. It was several days before I could delve into the daily musings from a time past. The empty house had a For Sale sign in the yard. I called Mom.

"Got some time today? I'm going to read the journals. Come over." She agreed and brought bagels and cream cheese, and I filled the coffee cups. "These books chronicle ten years. If there were other books before or after, they're lost or destroyed. A shame because her writings are a picture about life during that time."

"Well, let's dig in," Mom said, and we began to search for Dru. Mom quickly found a name she remembered, John Drew Stovall, a fellow banker and close friend of the family. "The old stories say he disappeared about the time Rachel and Logan got married. There was a fight I think."

"Here's what grandmother wrote," I read. *John D. argued, screaming. Punched Logan. John D. left. How can I choose?* She didn't waste words. Most writing was short sentences without adjectives. "A triangle. I love it, but Grandfather Logan won because that's who she married," my mystery senses on alert. "Do you remember John Stovall?"

"Sure, Grandmother Rachel talked about him some. He left and then came back."

"When? What year?"

"I don't remember. Grandfather Logan was furious because John D. opened a bank in Meadowbrook. Pulled away a lot of the farm business. I never knew him. Just heard all the talk."

"Do you think he's the Dru in the note and she changed the spelling? The poem from the wedding dress? And...what about the ticket to St. Louis?"

"Stop, please." Mom went silent, massaged her temples and tried to dredge up her memories. Suddenly, she threw her hands up in the air frustration written all over her face.

"I don't have any answers. Check the obits in the paper. He died a few years after he returned. I'm going to go play bridge." Mom gathered her things, stalked out of the house and slammed the door. Her bridge club was eight friends that did more talking than playing. Friendly gossip they called it.

I visited the library later in the week and enlisted the librarian's help. "Here it is," she said. "If I remember correctly, there's a side article about a fight over a woman just before he left town." I clamped my jaw shut, found both articles and printed them. On the way out I called Mom.

"It's time to finish reading. You won't believe what I've learned. Come to the house for lunch."

"Okay, I'm here. What'd you find?" Mom chewed a bite of turkey sandwich and drilled me with her eyes. I slid the papers in front of her.

"Logan and Drew were co-captains of the football team."

"That's right. Grandmother Rachel was the football queen."

I opened one of the journals and started to read. *Dru asked. Gave ticket to St. Louis. Leave tonight. Black eye, fight with Logan. Army enlistment. Dress ready.* Mom looked dumbfounded.

"Gimme that book. I don't believe this. She was going to run away with Dru?"

"Seems that way. The stub is torn, but she came back. And look at the dates. There are three days missing from the journal."

"All these years and I never knew." She slumped back against the chair. "Oh, my goodness. I almost didn't get born."

"That's about the size of it." I wrapped my arm around her shoulder. "Buried secrets from the attic. Sounds like a story to me," I said. "Let me tell you about my new mystery novel. It involves a triangle love affair."

"Kimberley, you can't do that, those are our family secrets, our dirty linen," she argued.

"Yeah, I know. Aren't families wonderful?"

NOT A SECOND TIME

Gary Fearon

I heard the song countless times growing up because the record got played a lot in my house. By the time I was four, I knew all the words, and whenever my grandmother came to visit, my parents had me sing it for her. I happily obliged, especially since my grandma took tremendous pleasure in singing along with me. I was five when I finally understood that she was in fact the person who recorded the song.

In the '50s, my grandmother went by the professional name Dina DeAngelis. She didn't use her real name, Denise Walker, because it didn't sound Italian. She was of German descent, but since some of the most popular male singers at that time were Italian, her manager's goal was for her to be the female Dean Martin.

While she was in her twenties, Dina had three Top 40 hits including her signature song "Love Will Be the Death of Me." A promotional tour in Italy and some sultry photo shoots succeeded in making her known as "The Menace from Venice," even though she was from Cleveland. In my youth, I thought she looked more glamorous than everyone else's grandmothers. When I became an adult, her old photos confirmed to me that she was hot stuff.

Dina enjoyed two years in the spotlight. Soon, her popularity faded when more approachable girl-next-door starlets like Doris Day and Sandra Dee were the next big thing. Dina became something of a joke in contrast, as fallen stars often do.

She died at 62 from liver failure, and I remember how upset my mother was that the tabloids jumped on that and built a story that Grandma had been an alcoholic. There were enough photos of her sporting glasses of wine to give those headlines credence. Eventually I, too, was convinced, and that became her new identity. I never held it against her, though. It provided a cautionary tale that kept me from ever developing a taste for alcohol, so that has been Grandma's prevailing legacy for me.

ର

I had just gotten home from work when my wife Nikki told me there was a message for me on the answering machine. It was brief and simply inquired as to whether I was a relative of Dina DeAngelis, and if so, to please return the call. The caller identified himself as the son of Leo Spear.

The name meant nothing to me, and to be honest, Nikki and I were hoping it was an attorney calling about a long lost will or something. However, a Google search revealed that Leo Spear had been a prominent manager for my grandmother and many other recording artists over the decades. I had heard of some, including one of Nikki's favorite bands, Fabulous Tomorrow.

"Thank you for getting back to me so soon," said Kevin Spear the next morning. "The reason I wanted to reach you is because they're coming out with a book about my father, Leo Spear. You may be aware that he died this year."

"I did see that. I'm very sorry."

"Thank you. He was a great guy. He and your grandmother were very fond of each other."

"Did you know my grandmother?"

"Not personally, but my dad talked about her a lot, especially after she died."

In my mind I calculated how many years ago that would have been. Roughly forty.

"I wish I remembered her better than I do," I said. "I didn't see much of her growing up."

"Well, she'll apparently be mentioned in this book," he continued. "A lot, in fact. And unfortunately, it won't be in the most favorable light."

I wasn't too surprised. "Seriously? Not the old alcohol thing again."

"Oh, that and much more, from what I hear. Do you know who

Al Goldberg is?"

"No idea."

"He's a celebrity biographer…the one who does those hatchet jobs. Wherever there's dirt he can dig up on a star, he buries them with it. And when he can't dig it up, he makes it up."

"So is he the one writing the book about your father?"

"Yeah. I got a heads-up from a friend who works for his publisher. She saw a rough draft and says it's full of illicit sex and drugs and other things I know can't be true. She said your grandmother will specifically be dragged through the mud with him."

"Grave robbers," I muttered. "I don't guess there's any way to stop it?"

"I asked my lawyer to issue a cease and desist order, but since my dad and Dina were public figures, he said the only thing to do is wait till it's published and hit them with defamation. Of course, by then the lies are already out there."

"When is this book coming out?"

"In three months. Now, I understand you're Dina's only living relative, right?"

"Now that you mention it, I guess I am."

"What I'm hoping is that you would be willing to join me in this defamation suit. It will have a lot more weight if both our names are on it."

"I've…never been part of anything like that," I said. "Can I think about it?"

"Of course. You have my number, but I'll be in touch too."

After we hung up and I explained the call to Nikki, I realized my hesitation in getting involved in a defamation suit is that I myself wouldn't know if the book contained lies or not. I never really knew my grandmother because she ended up moving to Italy, so I only saw her a few times as a kid. My parents would visit her over there while they were still alive, but I never made the trip with them.

The only real memories I have are the ones when we sang that song together. So I wasn't keen on getting embroiled in some legal thing that might come back to bite me.

My attic is a junkyard of holiday decorations, never-read books, dead computers, and boxes filled with items from when we emptied and sold my parents' house. I was in there to retrieve the books because Nikki wanted to go through them and donate some to the library, when I remembered that one of my parents' boxes contained some record albums. I wondered if my favorite song by my grandma was in there somewhere, and I brought that box down too.

Nikki sorted through the books while I riffled through the album jackets. Most of them were by artists I knew—Frank Sinatra, Ray Charles, The Monkees. A handful of LPs were bound together with rubber bands, which seemed like an odd thing to subject them to, but I was glad to see that the album on top was by Dina DeAngelis.

Removing the elastics gingerly, I scanned the back of the jacket to see if "Love Will Be the Death of Me" was on there, and indeed it was. I was grateful to still have a record player to play this treasure on.

I kept my fingers crossed that spending summers in a hot attic and being constricted by rubber bands hadn't damaged the decades-old LP. Fortunately, the vinyl looked good as new, and as I removed it from its cover, a piece of paper also slid out. It was a short handwritten note signed by Leo Spear.

> *Dina,*
>
> *Here's the 20th anniversary rerelease of your album. It looks like you've picked up some new fans as it's doing very well already. I'd send you a bottle of champagne if I thought you'd drink it!*
>
> *Best regards,*
>
> *Leo*

I read the note several times, assessing whether the champagne reference could be evidence that Grandma was or was not a drinker, but it could have meant any number of things. Some wine drinkers avoid champagne because it gives them headaches. But I did figure Kevin might like to have this handwritten note from his dad and planned to get his address next time we spoke.

To my relief, the LP was still in good condition. I played my favorite song to Nikki, who grinned to imagine my four-year-old self singing "Love Will Be the Death of Me".

We ended up listening to the entire album while we went through the box of books, and when it finished, I chose another LP from the previously bound collection. This was by another female singer named Priscilla Payne. As I removed that LP from its sleeve, another note dropped out.

Dina,

Let me know how you like Priscilla. She's an admirer of yours and I think she'll go far. She even reminds me of you.

I'd love to hear your thoughts in detail. Maybe make me one of those letter tapes like you've been sending to your daughter.

Fondly,

Leo

Clearly, these albums had belonged to my grandmother, and ended up at my parents' house. Hoping there might be more handwritten notes, I looked through the rest of the albums, and found none. But what was this about letter tapes?

My dad's old Pioneer tape recorder was another treasure in my attic next to a box full of tapes that I vowed to go through one day. Some were reel-to-reel versions of popular albums, but a few were home recordings.

Since my dad had been a ham radio enthusiast, I wasn't surprised that most of the 7-inch reels consisted of non-commercial broadcasts and various foreign transmissions taken directly off the air. I fast-forwarded through most of them.

It was upon playing the less conspicuous 3-inch reels that I was rewarded with the voice of my grandmother. I recognized her warm, melodic voice immediately as she dictated an audio letter to my mother. She spoke of everyday things as if she were on the phone, chatting away about life in Italy and how different authentic Italian food is. I smiled when she said she missed us and was looking forward to singing with me again someday.

There were six such tapes from Grandma, and Nikki and I listened intently for any mention of Leo Spear or something that might be helpful in debunking scandalous rumors. To our disappointment, the most controversial thing she spoke of was about trying a new hair color.

In my next conversation with Kevin, I told him about the notes I had found and asked if he'd like to have them. He appreciated the thought but said he had volumes of papers and things of his father's that he still had to go through. In the course of our conversation I also mentioned the letter tapes, and he perked up.

"What kind of tape were they on?" he asked.

"They were little 3-inch reels, why?"

"'Cause my dad has a ton of those! They might just be demo tapes or something, but I should see what's on them!"

We hung up quickly, and it was that evening when Kevin called back.

"You're not gonna believe this," he said. "There must be twenty of these tapes from your grandmother to my father."

"Have you listened to them?"

"Only a few so far, but I can't believe what I'm hearing! They're all so charming, so innocent. It's obvious she and my dad were just dear old buddies. She mentions that she and Priscilla Payne got to know each other and how lucky they both were to have a manager who never takes advantage of women. And you're gonna love this...she says how hilarious it is that 'The Menace from Venice' still has never touched a drop!"

"Are you kidding?" I exclaimed. "That's awesome!"

"It's true, my friend. *Thank you* for telling me about these tapes! I just spoke with my dad's lawyer and he says there might be enough ground to stop publication of that book."

Three months later, on what would have been the release date of the Goldberg tell-all, Kevin called to say he was writing his own biography of his father and incorporating many quotes from my grandmother's letter tapes.

He also gifted us with tickets to a reunion concert by Fabulous Tomorrow.

GRANDMOTHER'S GIFT

Nancy Roe

Millicent Payne celebrated her fiftieth birthday slumped on the couch in the same gray sweatpants she'd worn all week, watching *The Amazing Race,* eating a Little Caesars pepperoni pizza and a tray of six red velvet cupcakes from the grocery store. She'd always wanted to travel to exotic locations and fulfilled her fantasy by watching the reality TV show. How she wished she could compete. But fifty pounds overweight and unable to miss a day of work, it was only a dream.

A stack of overdue bills sat next to the pizza box. Clifford's cancer treatment had drained their savings. Then her husband drove his truck into a tree after a night of drinking with his buddies. The funeral, six weeks ago, only added to the pile of debt. Millicent hadn't paid the mortgage in almost a year and knew a foreclosure letter was imminent.

A week ago, she'd packed a few boxes. Not that she owned many valuables. Her late husband's mean streak that surfaced after a night of drinking led to broken or burned treasures. The only glimmer of goodness came from a high school friend who offered her a bedroom until she could get back on her feet.

A news preview caught her attention. A woman in California bought a painting at a thrift store that ended up being worth millions. *Lucky girl,* she thought. If only she were so lucky. She could pay off her debt, move to a new home with a swimming pool, and travel all over the world.

As Millicent drifted off to sleep, she pictured herself inside a hilltop mansion overlooking the Pacific Ocean. The west side of the brilliant white living room was one glass panel after another. White sectional couch, white coffee table, white drapes, and two white chairs. The only dash of color came from a sixteen-inch tall Chinese vase adorned with fish in vibrant orange, blue, and yellow.

Her grandmother appeared in a chair, waving a bamboo hand fan decorated with dark blue fish.

"My darling Millicent," Grandmother said. "The gift I gave you on your twenty-first birthday will wipe away your sadness. It's time for you to part with it. Take it to an auction house. It's not too late to live the life you've always imagined."

ॐ

During her shift at Walmart, Millicent thought about her dream. She couldn't remember the last time she'd seen the vase her grandmother had given her. She never liked the vase. *Too old for my taste.* But her grandmother had cherished it, and she cherished her grandmother and the story of the vase.

"For three years, your grandfather and I worked for the Clarks, a wealthy family in Atlanta. Your grandfather was so handsome in his butler's uniform, and he flirted with me as I cooked the family's meals. When we decided to marry, we asked the Clarks for a day off. The Clarks offered their gazebo for the ceremony, and they also provided all the flowers and food. Our wedding was the most perfect day. Their wedding gift to us was this Chinese vase. They told us that the vase would bring riches to the holder. My health is declining and I want to pass the vase and its wish to you. May this vase bring *you* riches."

Millicent knew she never would have parted with the vase. But where had she put it? Did her husband smash it against the wall in one of his rages? No, she would have put it somewhere safe. But where?

After her shift, she drove home and searched the entire house for the vase. The only treasure she found were two boxes of Girl Scout cookies she'd hidden behind her chest of drawers so Clifford wouldn't eat them.

She sat on the bed and opened the box of Thin Mints.

She'd finished the first sleeve and was halfway through the second one when she stood, hands on hips, and stared down the hall toward the living room. *Where is that darn vase?*

A light glowed above her head and she realized where she hadn't looked. *The attic.* The small cutout opening to the attic was hidden in her bedroom closet. The attic wasn't much more than a crawl space, but she'd been up there once, a few years after they moved in. Clifford had gone on a hunting trip, and she'd wanted to reorganize the closet without his interruption.

She brought in the ladder from the garage and put on rubber gloves. She shuddered at the thought critters might be skittering around, or worse—dead.

First, she needed to clear the closet shelf. She threw two boxes of dress shoes, a pillow, old sheets, and three sweatshirts that no longer fit to the floor. After three shoves, the ceiling cut-out moved, and she pushed it to the side.

Taking it slowly, she shined the flashlight in the attic, took another step on the ladder, and peeked inside. No furry or eight-legged creatures were in sight, but she spotted two bankers boxes. Two more steps on the ladder and she could sit on the attic floor. She crawled to the boxes, then pushed them toward the opening.

Millicent carried the boxes to the backyard. She feared a family of spiders had made their way inside the boxes and didn't want them loose in the house.

The first box contained old journals, photos of her parents, and her mother's recipe box. She said a brief prayer before lifting the second lid. *Please let the vase be in here.* Staring at her was Rudolph's face. *So that's where I put my favorite Christmas sweater.* She lifted the sweater and shook it. Out flew the gold ceramic handprint she made in second grade and it smashed into pieces. *Dagnabbit. You gotta be more careful.*

Next in the box were two flour sack kitchen towels. Her grandmother had stitched bouquets of colorful flowers in the corner. Millicent gently lifted the towels, not wanting to destroy anything that might be hidden between the folds. *Nothing.*

Her last hope rested underneath two layers of bubble wrap. Wrapped in sheets of tissue paper was her grandmother's vase.

ঌ

"Sold!" the auctioneer said as he banged the gavel.

Millicent sat in the front row, her eyes fixed on the auctioneer. Did she hear that right? There had been a bidding war on the vase. The vase that once belonged to an imperial family. The vase that came from the reign of the 18th-century emperor Qianlong. The vase that was estimated to sell between $1.3 million and $1.9 million. The vase that sold for $85 million.

"Congratulations, Millicent," the auctioneer said. "Mr. Clark is thrilled with his purchase."

"Mr. Clark? Is he here?" she asked, looking around the room.

"No. He lives in Atlanta and couldn't get away from his office. He made his bids over the phone."

Could it be? What are the odds he's a relative of the Clarks her grandmother worked for? "Please tell him I hope the vase brings him riches. I have a feeling he'll know what that means."

MERRY-GO-MURDER

Annette Cole Mastron

I gaze out the window and spot two red heads bobbing and weaving through the cotton fields, followed by Pastor Calvin walking toward my home.

I turn off my phone and meet Pastor Calvin on the front porch as my two red labs dance and jump around me with their tongues hanging out. I pet their heads, opening the door, and they scoot down the barn-wood floors toward the kitchen. I greet Calvin with a cheek peck and hug.

Calvin laughs and says, "Tractor and Trailer showed up at the church as I was preparing my sermon. I decided to come over to see how you're doing. It's been too long since we've talked."

"Come on in. You want coffee, tea or something stronger?" I ask as we walk down the dogtrot hall toward the kitchen. The pups lapped up all the water from their bowls. They are curled on top of their dog beds that sit on the brick window seats, overlooking the Mississippi River. It's their favorite spot in the house.

I refill their bowls and—looking out the kitchen window—glimpse my grandparent's home. It's where my uncle lived all of his life, except when he went to war. It's also where he was murdered.

I turn back to Calvin, gesturing towards the coffee pot, and he nods affirmatively. I pour a mug for us both. "Let's go out on the back porch," I say, handing him his steaming mug.

We sit in white rockers overlooking the pond and fenced community garden edged in marigolds and sunflowers. The river bend is just beyond the garden. Calvin gets right to the point. "I'm worried about you. Ever since your uncle died you haven't gone anywhere or seen your friends in the six months. You barely eat."

"That's not true." I whisper. "I've known you and your family my whole life. All my family is gone, and it's been very isolating. With my uncle's unsolved murder; Judge Fraierson and my cousins chomping at the bit to snatch the family land, inheritance taxes and trying to find a missing item…it's a lot."

"My family considers you family. Can we help?" he asks.

"I've just got to solve a couple of mysteries. The last time I saw my uncle was on this porch. I'd just bought a lottery ticket. I'd been to Memphis for a meeting with my attorney about the cousins' lawsuit. When I gassed up, I purchased a lottery ticket, I mean it had reached an obscene amount of money. I thought what the heck. We sat here and talked about what we'd do if we won. He told me he had the perfect place to keep the ticket safe. It never occurred to me that I'd never see him alive again."

"Wait, are you saying it was the winning ticket?" he looked shocked.

"It was. They identified the gas station, date and time it was purchased. I can't find the ticket, and for all I know my uncle's murderer took it."

"Wow."

"I know. It's a lot to process. With the ticket, I could right some wrongs in our community. I've not told anyone about this and would appreciate your confidence."

Late afternoon turned to dusk. Pastor Calvin said goodbye. I promise him to eat something. I think, "Does half a sleeve of Ritz crackers count?"

As I leave my home the next day, I wave at Pastor Calvin. The monthly baptisms are taking place in my pond. At least ten white-robed converts are being baptized today. The church ladies are setting up a luncheon under the cottonwood trees. I wave at Miss Mimi who is directing the activity. She waves back.

With my snake hoe in hand and rain boots on, I cut through the woods and come to the clearing connecting my land to my grandparent's land. I walk past the family plot dating back to the 1700's. I pass the 100-year-old barn I played in as a child. My grandparent's home, a faded white Victorian, sits high on a bluff facing the Mississippi River.

I put down my hoe and take the keys out of the pocket of my crossbody bag. Although I'm not Catholic, I believe in the power of prayers to various saints for various human needs. They are some of the most poetic prayers. I say the St. Anthony's prayer out loud.

As I say "Amen," I open the exterior door, step into the airlock and relock the security door. I insert the 130-year-old skeleton key and open the stain glass door to enter the parlor.

The antique, mahogany secretary sits as a focal point in the room. It has a secret compartment that only I know about, since everyone else that once knew are dead.

I move the ladder-back chair and sit in front of the secretary. Both the secretary and chair came to live in this relic of a home after falling off a train when it was loaded improperly. They were rescued by my grandfather. I open the secretary's slanted front which creates a desktop when pulled down.

The secret compartment on the left holds the attic key. My previous search did not result in finding the ticket. I close the compartment and the desk.

I walk through the double French doors to the ladies parlor and climb the worn oak stairs. I pause at the landing, bending down to glimpse the Mississippi River through the only clear pane in the huge flower bouquet depicted in the stain glass window. It's something I've always done since I was tall enough to peek through the clear glass. There were two speedboats on the river and a loaded barge heading south.

The stair landing, though clean now, was where my uncle was found shot in the head. I climb to the third floor and unlock the attic door. The dismal gray of the day permeates the attic. The skylight provides limited light. I look around at the attic and see remnants of my father, uncle and my childhood. At one end, there are a collection of trunks and luggage from various relatives. There is a roll top desk I've already searched. No hidden compartments found. I even googled the desk to see if anyone knew of hidden compartments like in that treasure hunter movie.

I sit on the wooden window seat looking the length of the attic to the matching window seat at the far end of the house. I hope to spot any obvious cracks or crevices that could be hiding a slim piece of paper. There are so many options it seems like a lost cause. Come on, St. Anthony.

My phone barks, I recognize the number. "This should be good," I think. I answer.

"Whatcha doing?" he says.

"Nothing much, you?"

"Thought you'd wanna meet and bury the hatchet. I know we lost in court. Can we be kissing cousins, again? Want to meet at the Blue & White cafe?"

"Ew," I think. Out loud I say, "we were never kissing cousins, and a meeting without $1000 an hour attorneys, not gonna happen."

"You gonna hold a grudge for forever?"

"To hold a grudge means I care what you think and I don't." I hang up and text my attorney about the call just to keep him in the loop. My cousin doesn't do anything without a motive. Wonder what he's up to?

Again, I focus on the attic contents to search. My dad's train layout is here, like it's still waiting on him. Maybe it's in one of the trains? No, my uncle would pick something that was his, not my dad's.

I look at my dollhouse, an exact replica of this home. It was my birthday gift on my 6th birthday. My uncle carved it and the furniture. I spent hours playing with it during my childhood. I bend over, looking through the house. I carefully pick it up to see if the ticket is underneath.

The sun pops through the clouds, light fills the attic and lights up a carved merry-go-round on the highboy storage bookcase. I don't remember ever seeing it before. I rise on my tiptoes to pick up the merry-go-round. It looks like it's hand carved like my dollhouse. I wonder. My hand bumps something metal at the back corner of the shelf. I hold the merry-go-round in one hand and pull the metal lever. The entire bookcase opens quietly towards me. "Woah!" I say out loud to no one but me. The house has relinquished a secret to me. I peek inside the opening I never knew existed.

Suddenly, I hear a noise outside the attic window. Looking down, I see my two cousins at the top of the stairs coming up the bluff from the banks of the river. I zoom in with my phone camera and take a couple of pictures. I wonder if they were one of the boats I had seen earlier on the river. He must have called me from the water. I know I locked the security door when I came in. I should be okay.

As a precaution, I call the private security company that monitors our properties. I text them their picture and request they call the sheriff. When I disconnect the phone, the house groans with the sound of glass breaking.

I decide to step through the bookcase and close it behind me. I can't believe I never knew it was here waiting for me. Much like the main attic, it stretches from one end of the house to the other with matching skylights. There are no exterior windows like in the main attic.

I set the merry go-round on the work table littered with carved circus and carnival figures. Inspecting the merry-go-round, I discover a lever much like in the bookcase, only smaller. I pull the lever and a drawer pops out. Sitting all alone is the lottery ticket. I google the lottery website and check the numbers to the ticket. Yes, it is the winning ticket!

On the table, I see a small sealed plastic bag of dollhouse size lights. I dump the lights onto the table and place the lottery ticket inside the bag, squeezing all the air out and sealing it shut. I pop off my phone case decorated with banned book titles and place the plastic sealed ticket inside before reattaching the case to my phone. I take a few pictures of my uncle's hidden workshop cave.

I hear voices coming up the stairs, so I check my phone to make sure the ringer is turned off. I send another text to my attorney letting him know my two cousins broke into the house. I creep to the bookcase wall, so I can hear them. I turn up the volume and hit voice record. My two cousins, nicknamed Dumb and Dumber, enter the attic.

"I thought you said you saw her go in the house."

"I did while you were on the phone."

"Clearly, she's not here. If she were, I'd kill her for hanging up on me. What a witch."

"Maybe she went out the back door toward the road."

"Naw, Billy Parker's watching the road, he called and said the security system was alerted by her, so she has to be here."

I cover my mouth to stop a gasp. Billy is the county sheriff. That explains some things. I never thought my cousins were a physical threat. I just thought they had a mean streak.

"We've been through that desk a gazillion times, there is no money in it. He had tons of money so where is it? I'll bet she has it by now."

"You should never have pushed him down the stairs."

"Well, you shot him in the head."

"Shut up."

Stunned but silent, I sit in my uncle's safe room, letting their confession wash over me. They killed him for money. Ironic. The night I bought the ticket, we talked of all the lives we would change with the winnings, if we won. Dumb and Dumber were high on the list because, as my uncle said, they weren't raised right and always seemed to struggle.

I hear footsteps moving toward the luggage part of the attic. Voices become muffled. I stay where I am.

I send another text including the voice recording of their confession to my attorney. A reply text tells me the state police are on the way and to stay hidden.

My last text of the evening is to Pastor Calvin. I fill him in on everything and send the confession to him, asking for his help.

Ten minutes seems like ten hours.

I hear barking and a loud commotion. The cousins start freaking out. I hear them apparently stumble down the attic staircase. Barking turns to growling. I stick my phone in my right boot, searching for the release on the safe room side of the bookcase. I see a matching lever and pull. The bookcase opens in reverse to the main attic. I close it, just as Tractor and Trailer leap off the top attic step towards me. I pet them and praise them for being such good dogs.

Pastor Calvin pops up the stairs. "You alright, now?"

I nod yes and tears roll down my cheeks. "Thank you."

We leave the attic and find Pastor Calvin's entire congregation in my grandparents' parlor with people flowing out through the airlock onto the front porch. Miss Mimi sits in the ladder-back chair directing the detainment of my murdering cousins.

The state police arrive, taking my cousins into custody. An arrest warrant is issued for the sheriff.

Now, my attorney is helping me navigate this unexpected windfall. I've written out all the suggestions my uncle and I discussed on his last night before our lives changed forever. His last wishes will be honored. I'm thinking of using some of the winnings to donate a life-sized merry-go-round in the town square. It seems to be my good luck talisman.

In reflection, it occurs to me, our lives are like a merry-go-round. Our choices flow around us, we can get on or off, go up and down or just sit as we spin through our lives.

THE HOMECOMING

Ronald Lloyd

Turning off the gravel country road and into the driveway, Amanda and her mother, Mary, looked up at the house on top of the hill and grimaced. It was a two-story, brick colonial which had fallen into disrepair, its shutters askew and shingles hanging from the eaves. Looking at her mother, Amanda raised an eyebrow. "Is this it?"

"I'm afraid so. You should have seen it when my father was alive. It was the showplace of the county." Shaking her head, she added, "I can't believe this."

Focusing on the rutted gravel driveway, Amanda muttered, "I can" as she approached the house. In Amanda's estimation, her mother's sister had always been the crazy spinster aunt.

"Pardon?"

Busy fighting potholes and ruts, she said, "Oh, nothing."

When Amanda parked beside the house, her mother clucked her tongue twice in disbelief. "This wouldn't have happened if my brother Tom had been here."

The subject of the long-gone uncle having always been "verboten", Amanda took the plunge. "Did he really just leave without a word?"

"Apparently. At least that's what my sister told me, but it was two years after my father died and right after my mother passed. Plus, I was married, so I wasn't around."

Pressing her opportunity, Amanda continued, "And you've not heard anything since?"

"No, not a thing."

"Any idea why he left?"

"Well, I have my suspicions...."

"And?"

Seeing her mother's jaw tighten, Amanda feared she had gone

too far, but relenting, her mother said, "Like I said, I only have suspicions, but I think my brother felt Madge was smothering him. At least, at mom's funeral, he mentioned moving away." Then with a laugh added, "Boy, was Madge upset. She began to rant, shouting that she wouldn't let him leave."

After a reflective pause, she continued, "I guess it got to the point that the only way he felt he could have his own life was to run away and never come back. Who knows?"

Pointing to the house, Amanda asked, "Is that going to be a problem?" hastily adding, "Ya know, the inheritance and everything?"

Tilting her head to the side, her mother admitted, "I suppose." Turning to look at her daughter, she continued, "After Tom was gone a few years, I wanted to hire a detective to look for him, but Madge was adamant. She said that it was better to let sleeping dogs lie and when he wanted to contact us, he would, but I always wondered."

Twisting in her seat, Amanda asked, "Do you have the key?"

After digging around inside her purse, her mother announced, "Here it is," adding, "When the nurse at the home gave me Madge's effects, it was on the top."

Blinking away tears, she continued, "She wasn't much of a sister. I was lucky to get a ten-minute phone call once or twice a year, but she was still my sister."

Looking up at the rotten screens hanging in strips from the windows of the side porch, she continued, "I just realized this is the first time I've been back to the farm since my mother died."

Reaching down, she pulled on the door handle as she said, "The one time I saw Madge after mom passed, she insisted on coming to our house. She said it would give her an excuse to come to the city."

After they both stepped out of the car, Amanda came around to stand shoulder to shoulder with her mother. Taking a deep breath, she nodded toward the house and asked, "Alright mom, are you ready?" At a nod from her mother, they started up the walk together.

Standing on the bottom of the porch's three wooden steps,

Amanda's mother yanked on the screen door, but it didn't budge. Tugging harder a second time, it still didn't move. Looking back at her daughter, she said, "It's stuck."

"I'll get a tire iron."

When Amanda pried on the light wooden frame, it sprang open, falling to the side and swaying on one hinge. For a moment, neither woman moved, eyeing the tottering door suspiciously. When the door didn't fall, Amanda ascended the steps, pushing the screen to the side as she entered. "Watch out," her mother said, "the porch floor might be rotten."

Once inside the house, her mother flipped a remembered light switch, but nothing happened. "I guess no one paid the electric bill while Madge was in the nursing home."

Taking out their cellphones, both slid a finger up from the bottom of the screen, bringing up a series of apps. When they tapped on the flashlight icon two beams of light pierced the darkness, illuminating a small table on the left side of the hall. On the table was a large color photograph of a smiling red-haired boy, flanked by two candles, hardened wax hanging precariously down the side of each. With a shiver, Amanda reflected that the table and photo looked exactly like those cult shrines you see in horror films.

Pointing at the picture, Amanda asked, "Who's that?"

"Tom, my brother."

"Strange."

"Yeah."

Amanda considered leaving the tire iron at the entrance but seeing the shrine decided to keep it. Everything about this place made her nervous.

Dropping the beam to the floor, Amanda walked past the table, entered the living room, and gasped. If the table and the photo had been bazaar, what greeted them here was a scene right out of a psychology textbook. Boxes, plastic bags, piles of old newspapers, and nearly anything else you could imagine were piled on dust-covered furniture, rising in some places to the ceiling.

Between the towers of detritus were narrow spaces forming aisles that serpentined across the room. The piles had fallen over in several places clogging the passageways, but a few remained clear enough for a person to edge sideways between the mounds.

Afraid of being inundated by an avalanche, mother and daughter cautiously crossed the room. Stopping in front of a window, her mother reached up and grasped the drapes. As she yanked them open, her fingers penetrated the fabric, tearing holes in the cloth.

As dirt cascaded down on them, Amanda and her mother backed away, covering their faces. Once free of the cloud, the two women stood, coughing and spluttering, furiously brushing grime from their clothes.

Swinging her hands in an arch, Amanda asked, "What are you going to do with all this?"

With a raise of her eyebrows her mother said, "I don't think we have much choice. We can't sell the house until we hire some men to haul all this junk away."

"This place gives me the creeps. Why don't we leave it for the cleaners?"

Pivoting, her mother agreed, "I would love to, but there are some things from my childhood I don't want to be thrown away by mistake. Come on. The sooner we finish, the sooner we get out of here."

Raising her light, Amanda turned left, following her mother down another trail. Once past an archway, Amanda found herself in the dining room, the table and chairs filled and overflowing with still more rubbish. As her mother rounded the table, she brushed a pile of yellowing mail, one piece falling to the floor. On impulse, Amanda bent and, picking it up, saw it was an advertisement for a sale at Walmart, over ten years old. Following her mother around the table heaped to the chandelier, Amanda was surprised to find a small empty space burrowed into the mound.

Perplexed, she pondered the cleared space until it abruptly came to her. This was where her aunt ate her meals. Hearing hinges squeal, Amanda looked up to see her mother push open a swinging door. Realizing this must be the kitchen, Amanda turned to follow but was almost bowled over as her mother backpaddled, the reek of rotting food pursuing her.

Scrunching up their noses at the smell, both retreated to the living room. Frowning, Amanda asked, "What are you going to do about that?"

"We'll leave it for later. On the way out, I'll open the kitchen door from the outside and let it air out."

"Okay, what's next?"

She pointed to the stairs on the other side of the room. "Up there, I suppose."

Once up the stairs, her mother stopped in the middle of the hall. Pointing to the left, she said, "That was my parents' room," then turning, she pointed to the other side. "That was Madge and my room." Pivoting, her mother gestured at an extra-large pile of boxes at the end of the hall. "Behind those are the stairs into the attic. Tom's room was up there."

Stepping across the hall, her mother opened her sister's room and froze. Peering around her, Amanda saw that unlike the rest of the house, this room was spotless.

"I don't get it. Why is this room different?"

"I guess she had to have one place she could live."

After a cursory inventory of the room, Amanda's mother said, "There is nothing here I want. Let's go."

With a nod, Amanda followed her but as they entered the hall, she absently swung her light toward the pile of trash at the far end and saw a metallic glint. Holding the light on the metal she asked, "What's that?"

Shaking her head, her mother said, "Don't know," as she walked toward the end of the hall.

After pulling several trash bags off the mound, her mother stepped back, and looking at the hasp and the large padlock she had revealed near the top, said, "Weird." Plucking more bags and boxes away from the door, she revealed a second metal hasp and padlock near the bottom.

Turning to her daughter, she asked, "What do you think?"

Pointing the tire iron at the top hasp, Amanda replied, "We've come this far."

Sliding the beveled tip of the iron between the latch and the door, Amanda pulled, but nothing happened. Pressing her foot against the doorsill, she used her leg muscles to pry on the hinge until, with a screech, the small cheap screws of the top hasp pulled out of the wood.

After repeating the process on the bottom fastener, Amanda reached out, turned the doorknob, and pulled. Rusty hinges protesting, Amanda opened the door and peered up the short stairway.

Shining her light into the darkness, Amanda saw chunks of wallpaper hanging from the sloped wall of the attic above her. Ascending first one step and then another, she halted, her eyes even with the attic floor.

Looking to the right, she saw a small chest of drawers with a dust obscured mirror above it. Beside the chest was a free-standing rack with clothes still on the rusty wire hangers.

Turning to the left, she shined her light on a narrow bed, a handmade quilt hanging over the side. Ascending to the third step, her head rose high enough to see over the edge of the bed. With the light of her phone beginning to pale, she could just distinguish a long lump under the quilt.

Moving the weakening beam up to the head of the bed, a shiver went down her spine when she saw a skull, red hair splayed out on the pillow underneath it. Erect in an eye socket was the handle of an ice pick.

Frozen in disbelief, Amanda didn't move or speak. Her mother, a quiver in her voice, asked, "What is it? What do you see?"

"It's your brother."

THE SUITCASE FULL OF MEMORIES

Karen Busler

"Girls! What are you doing in the attic?" I scolded my granddaughter and her friends. "It's dirty and you could get hurt up there."

"Hi Gram! We're playing with all these old clothes we found in this suitcase up here. Did you know these were here? Who wore these flowery jeans? And look at the hats and scarves." Then her eyes got wide and asked, "Were these yours?"

I had to smile. My thirteen-year-old granddaughter Cara was insatiable in wanting to know everything about what interested her. She was definitely the ringleader of her two best friends, Sophie and Emily.

"Why would you think all that stuff is mine?" I teased them.

Cara stood up to her full 5 foot 6 inch height and challenged me, "Why else would they be here? They've got to be yours, or costumes!"

I laughed at her correct deduction and said, "Yep, those are mine. But I really don't want you girls playing up in the attic. There're nails and unfloored areas and you might get hurt. But I'll tell you what, bring the suitcase downstairs and I'll tell you stories about some of these clothes."

"Okay!!" they squealed together.

After wrestling the big suitcase down to the living room, the curious girls started pulling everything out one by one, amazed at what they saw.

"Did you really wear these funny looking jeans? Why are the bottoms of the legs so big?" Emily wanted to know.

Ah, the ignorance of the new generation about what we oldsters thought was hip when we were young.

"I'll have you know those jeans were the absolute grooviest things a girl could wear. They're called hip hugger bell-bottoms, and to make the bells even bigger, we'd split the seams open and sew in the flowery material. We'd also sew embroidered butterflies on the back pockets and flowered patches all over them. See, right there? And we'd wear crop tops with the low cut jeans," I said, pulling out my favorite chartreuse halter top and waving it around.

"Gram! I can't believe you'd wear this. You'd show your whole tummy and back!" Cara said with her jaw hanging open.

I grinned at her, "That's what we all did back in the '60s. My mother sure didn't like it much, but I wasn't about to wear a sweater set, poodle skirt, and saddle oxfords from the '50s and look like a total nerd. Oh, here's the topper to it all," I said as I found my favorite orange and white wide-brimmed floppy hat.

"You've got to be kidding!" Sophie said, but she put it on and sashayed around the room, wiggling like a bad disco dancer while we howled with laughter.

"Can I put this on, Gram?" Cara pleaded.

"Sure, but I thought you thought this wasn't cool," I said.

"Well, I won't go out in this, I just want to see what it looks like on."

"Fine with me, but let me get my camera while you change."

She had no idea of why I kept those particular clothes but they meant a lot to me. But Cara meant even more so I didn't mind. I might even put a picture of her in them next to the one of me in the same clothes. She'd appreciate it later.

Cara grabbed the jeans, crop top, a long scarf and hat, and ran to change.

"Are you ready?" she yelled from her bedroom and her friends made some unintelligible noise to answer but sounded affirmative. I was also ready to capture this moment for posterity.

"WAIT!" I yelled. "You've got to have some music for this fashion blast from the past."

"Okay, but hurry," Cara yelled back.

I quickly found one of my favorite records, Starship's *We Built This City,* and put it on. It was perfect.

Then I announced, "And now, straight from the '60s, heeere's Cara!"

Always the little actress with perfect timing, Cara waited for the music introduction to finish before she stepped out into the room to the pulsing beat. Sophie and Emily's eyes nearly popped out of their heads when they saw Cara in her "flower power" outfit, moving effortlessly to the beat of the music. A tear ran down my face but I quickly brushed it away. I had to capture this for posterity and had no time to think of my own past.

Cara's friends jumped up and started dancing with her on the living room "runway" having the time of their lives. They pulled me into the fray as I continued recording them.

When the song was over and we all collapsed, heaving to get air, the rolling-on-the-floor laughing started.

"That was AWESOME," Cara whooped. "These clothes make me feel like a superstar! No wonder you kept them, Gram."

Emily coughed, "What else do you have in that suitcase?"

"All kinds of ancient stuff that was fun to wear," I said.

Cara stood, and holding out her hands demanded, "But I still want to know why you kept all this stuff."

My granddaughter's question brought back other old feelings that I'd pushed aside years ago.

"Well?" Cara insisted, after I waited too long to answer.

"Do you really want to know these stories?" I asked them.

"YES!" was the shouted unanimous answer. I had to smile, which made them even more adamant.

"Okay, I'll tell you the tale of why I kept these things."

They settled down on the floor next to the suitcase and I got comfortable in a big chair. This was going to be hard for me but I did want them to know what life was like back then, though not necessarily what I went through.

"Once upon a time ..." The kids all groaned and gave me stinky looks. "I'm sorry, I couldn't resist! Okay, here's the real deal.

"Long before I met Cara's granddad, I was a senior in high school dating a boy named Jimmy. We were inseparable. Of course, this was back at the height of the Vietnam War and we were all terrified that the draft would take our guys into that war. Well, Jimmy's number did come up and he was drafted. After his basic training he and a lot of our friends were shipped out to Vietnam.

"I have to tell you it was not a good time. I wrote to him every day, hoping that at least a few letters would get through to him." I reached into the suitcase again and pulled out a small stack of envelopes tied with a ribbon. "These are the few letters I got from Jimmy."

The girls were silent. They didn't want to think of what might come next. I pulled a flowing psychedelic skirt out of the suitcase and held it up. "This was the skirt I wore when Jimmy went off to war. He said when he came home, he wanted me to wear it so he could find me fast in the crowd. He didn't want to waste a minute of not being with me."

The girls reverently passed it from one to the other and then back to me. I folded it and put it across my lap.

"As you might be guessing by now, Jimmy never came back. He went MIA and was never found."

I had to pause for a minute. The fear I had experienced came back in a tiny wave. At least it was only a shadow of what I went through at that time.

"Gram? Were you going to marry him?" Cara asked in her innocence.

"Yes, we were going to get married as soon as he got back. But of course that never happened. To answer your next question you haven't asked yet, yes, your granddad knows all this. In fact, he's the one who helped me get through my grief and brought me back to life. And I love him for that as well as all his other good qualities. Besides, YOU wouldn't be here if I hadn't married my Grant!"

Cara and her friends giggled at that, lightening the mood.

"Those clothes you have on, Cara, are what I wore when Jimmy proposed. So they're very special to me."

Cara traced the flower design in the bell-bottoms with her finger and pondered on that for a second. Before she could say anything I said, "We had some mighty good times in all these clothes, dancing the night away. We absolutely adored dancing and went as often as we could."

"Granddad likes dancing, too. Did you think about Jimmy when you were dancing with Granddad?" Cara asked.

"Such a grownup question!" I said, raising my eyebrows. "But here's the answer. At first I did, and Granddad knew it, but he persisted in winning me over and making my memories hurt a lot less. Now when we go dancing, all I think about is your wonderful grandfather!"

"I sure hope you do!" came a booming voice from the doorway. All of us jumped because we didn't hear Grant come in.

"Sweetheart! You startled all of us! I was just telling them the stories about some of these old clothes."

"Ah yes, lots of good memories," Grant said with a slight smile. "But I heard some Starship earlier and had to see what was going on in here. I see that Cara has decided to become a hippie!"

It was funny seeing Cara look at him like he had four heads. She was clueless as to what a hippie was.

"Don't worry about that," I laughed. "Hippie times are over. Who wants to dance to *Footloose*?"

Grant perked up and the girls looked clueless again. "You three have a lot to learn, so we'd better get to it!" I said.

I put *Footloose* on the record player and Grant and I showed them how to dance the dances we did back in the '60s and '70s. I looked at my husband with such love, silently communicating with him about how much I appreciate the man he is. He helped me heal, and he knew it and loved me all the more for who I've become.

"Come on Gram, put on your hippie hat and shake it!"

Ahh, youth.

Later that night when all was quiet, Grant and I folded the clothes and put them in the suitcase to go back in the attic.

"You did a fine job of explaining these clothes to the girls, Sweetheart, and I'm glad you didn't tell them our secrets about them, even though some of your story had a little truth to it," Grant said with a smile.

"Well, I was put on the spot and had to come up with something fast!" I said. "Even those old letters you wrote to me helped to make the ruse more believable. I'm just glad they didn't ask to read them! And just in case Cara gets curious later, I think I'll destroy them, but only if that's okay with you."

"That's fine. It's such ancient history, and we know what happened. Nobody else needs to know," Grant said, hugging me tight. After a minute he held up the psychedelic skirt and said, "You were wearing this when I found you, all huddled up in a ball, scared to death in that gazebo in the park."

"Yes, and you *did* save me from that awful Jimmy, trying his best to get me addicted to his drugs. You were my hero then, and you'll always be my hero! Your humility inspires me, not wanting anyone to know what you did for me. And the best part is, you *did* help me heal - from my insecurities, seeing the good in me and encouraging me, and mainly getting Jimmy gone from our lives."

"It was my pleasure, my Love. Dance with me?"

"Always," I said.

Grant took me in his arms and we swayed to the beat of our matching drummers.

CAT TAG

Frank DiBianca

"Will it ever end?" George groaned, as he and Melinda Saunders, both young retirees thanks to several of Melinda's fantastic stock purchases, sat at their kitchen table drinking second cups of coffee like they did every Saturday morning.

"You've been staring at that to-do list and mumbling for half an hour. What's the problem now?" Melinda put her pencil down and dipped her head toward her husband.

"The furnace is yakking. My brakes are squealing. The overhead lights in the hallway started flickering. Everything's just fine."

She looked up at him. "What's an eight-letter word for 'exhibit displeasure?'"

George smiled in triumph. "Complain!"

"Now isn't *that* appropriate?" Melinda shot back. She picked up her pencil and wrote the answer into her crossword puzzle.

"Hmph. Well, at least my built-in-shelves project is finished," he added with an air of finality.

But Melinda ignored him and put forward *her* closer. "Good. Now we have someplace to put all the junk that's been gathering dust for decades in those boxes in the attic."

George grabbed his list and stomped out.

He couldn't win them all, Melinda thought as she entered a few more words into her crossword and walked over to the refrigerator. After taking out a half-filled bottle of sparkling grape juice and grabbing two glasses, she meandered down the hall to the family room. Placing the glasses on the coffee table, she filled them and put one on the end table next to the almost-flat recliner where her husband, now dead to the world, lay unaware of her presence.

After returning to the coffee table and taking a long drink of her beverage, Melinda made herself comfortable on her recliner and was soon asleep herself.

ർ

George, lost in dreamland, was on his knees in the attic, and Melinda was holding his head by both ears inside a murky box of paraphernalia, while her words echoed throughout the dark room. "Why did you dump me and take Hottie Heather Wicker to the Senior Prom? . . . Why did you dump me and take…" Then he faintly heard the alarm of his cellphone which he'd left on the end table and realized he'd been asleep. He picked it up just as Melinda jerked herself up on the recliner and turned to him.

"Hello," George answered. As the caller spoke, George frowned and pointed to Melinda and then to his ear to indicate he wanted her to hear the caller. He tapped the face of his phone to activate the speaker. "Yes, that's our phone number. May I help you, ma'am?" George gave Melinda a big shrug.

"I live near the Highwood Retirement Village, and my daughter Annie just found a young cat. It has a cat tag with your phone number and the name Sadie on it. She wants to keep it, but my husband is allergic to cats. I'm wondering if you would like to see the cat and the tag with your phone number. How far away are you from Highwood?"

"About ten minutes. Please hold on for a minute while I talk to my wife about this. Thank you."

By this time, Melinda had moved to a chair closer to George. "Wow. This is wild."

"What do you think, honey?"

"I'm dying to see the tag *and* the cat," Melinda replied. "We've never had one since my Tipsy died when we were first married. What's a ten-minute drive?"

ർ

A few minutes later, the Saunders parked near the front entrance to Highwood as had been agreed on the phone. They walked a few hundred feet to a middle-aged woman and a young, teary-eyed preteen hugging a tan cat with black spots and somewhat large ears.

The mother held out her hand. "Hi, I'm Dianne Bennett. This is Annie and her friend, Sadie." At this, Annie burst into sobbing.

"Annie, I know this is hard for you," said her mother. "Please give me the cat and sit on the steps over there." She pointed to a brick staircase a short distance away.

The Saunders introduced themselves, and after a bit of chit-chat, the discussion began.

"So, a couple of hours ago, Annie, who was on our backyard swing, came in with this beautiful animal. Here, take a look at her tag."

"Look at that," Melinda said, "the area code is right too."

"I don't see how the owners could have put the wrong phone number on her. Do you have any friends who like to play practical jokes?" Dianne overlapped her lips.

"Not this kind," George answered. "But I have a strange feeling. I think this cat was meant for us. Plus, we don't have any cat allergies. If we take her, and things don't work out, we'll find her a good owner. Whadaya say, Melinda?"

"Dianne, do you know anything about this type of cat?"

"How funny you should ask, Melinda. While I was waiting for you, my cell phone and the internet made me a cat expert. I'm almost certain Sadie is a Savannah. They are large, affectionate, intelligent animals."

Melinda turned to George and smiled. "Let's do it!" Then she walked over to the youngster while George and Dianne exchanged contact information. "Annie, I promise you we'll be good to Sadie. And guess what? You can come over to see her anytime your parents will let you. How does that sound?"

Annie jumped up and gave Melinda a huge hug. And a kiss.

ঌ

On the way home, the Saunders stopped at a pet store and

bought Sadie food, supplies, some bowls, and a cat bed. They also picked up a book on cat ownership. After a short ride, they were back in their home, and Sadie was on the floor exploring the terrain.

The cat quickly did a disappearing act, and after a game of hide and seek, had to be coaxed out from under the master bed.

"I'm hungry," George said. "What do we have for lunch, Babe?"

"If you'll microwave the frozen enchilada dinners, I'll put some cat food and water in Sadie's bowls, and we can have a nice family dinner. How's that, Mr. Handyman?"

"Fine. And since we're discussing food, I wonder if Sadie is housebroken."

Melinda gave her head a toss. "Well, we can take her outside into our wonderful backyard after lunch."

After lunch and a successful restroom break, George and Melinda took turns on the floor playing with their new friend, who needed a while to warm up to them. Sadie's reticence was slowly eased by the periodic administration of cat treats, until she finally let herself be petted.

Late in the afternoon, after Melinda had perused the cat book, the couple settled into their recliners in the family room to plan Sadie's first night in her new home.

"The book says the cat can sleep in her own room," Melinda said, "if she's secure and has a nice bed and blanket. That's what we always did with Tipsy."

George tapped his chin with his fist. "Hmm . . . she's sure not gonna sleep in our bedroom. And I'm not comfortable about leaving her on the main floor with all the furniture and carpets. Don't cats scratch a lot?"

"They do, according to the book, although we didn't have much of a problem with Tipsy." Melinda snapped her fingers and made a grunt. "Darn it. I saw a cat scratching post at the pet shop. Should we go back and get one?"

George glanced at his watch. "Nope. Sign said they close at five.

It's 4:55. Anyway, it's not just the scratching. Who knows what else she might do with the stuff we have on this floor. It's the attic or the basement."

"Not the attic, with all those boxes of junk and papers. I guess it's the basement, right?"

"Yep. It's your turn to cook dinner. How about if I take her and her bed downstairs? We can play and explore. Get her accommodated there. Maybe reduce the mouse and bug population a bit." George chuckled.

"Very funny."

After dinner, the two of them took Sadie back to the basement and played some more with her. When it got dark, they put the cat bed on the exercise mat. Then they put Sadie in her bed and they both lay on the mat, making snoring sounds. Sadie left the bed. They kept putting the cat in bed, and the cat kept getting out.

Finally, Melinda got up and turned to George. "Why don't you run around with her. If she gets tired, maybe she'll go to sleep."

So, George got up. First he walked around carrying Sadie. Then he put Sadie on the floor and jogged with her. Then he ran. After each jaunt, they put her in bed and did the snoring act. Nothing worked. Next, he tried running at her, and she finally began scampering away. But each time Sadie refused to stay in bed.

"My last idea, and then we go upstairs. I'll act crazy." He got up and ran around, waving his arms. Then he ran straight at the furnace and made a quick stop to turn back. But he slipped and stumbled headlong toward the wall. Only by grabbing a pipe did he avoid a bad injury. "That does it," he said, after regaining his composure. "Let's go before I kill myself. Sadie knows where the bed is if she cares to sleep in it. Otherwise the mat or the floor will do fine."

They ran up the stairwell, opened the door, flipped off the light switch, and quickly closed the door, just as the cat was making a beeline toward them.

After all their exertion, the couple was soon in bed and fast asleep.

ꟹ

At 2:30 a.m., George woke up as usual. As he walked toward the master bathroom, he heard a faint cat cry from the hall outside the open door. He rushed into the hall and ran toward the basement door at the far end. As he neared the door, the meowing got progressively louder. Upon opening the door, Sadie, who'd been crying for help, jumped up onto the main floor and ran down the hall.

A quick sniff explained everything. "Gas Leak! Gas Leak!" George screamed with all his might, and he hesitated for only a moment to evaluate which order of events was best. He flipped on the basement light switch, ran downstairs to the furnace, and closed the main gas shut off valve. Then he turned off the electrical power to the furnace and hot water heater and threw open two outside windows high on the basement wall to let fresh air in.

In a few seconds he was back at the bedroom door just as Melinda was coming out in her nightgown.

"Gas leak! Grab a coat and your shoes!" George yelled. "Go! Go! Go!"

ꟹ

Twelve hours later, after calling the fire department and gas company and getting a few more hours of sleep at a nearby motel, the unharmed threesome were back at home. The gas company had left a note saying they'd fixed the moderate gas leak, and the safety measures the owners had taken before they arrived were crucial in preventing a gas explosion.

"How about that." George had just read the note to his wife as the couple lay on their recliners. "Sadie saved our lives, and I saved our house."

"Yeah, and I saved Sadie," said Melinda as she turned and smiled at the cat, who meowed and continued munching her treats.

ණ

By the next day, life at the Saunders home had settled down once more. Melinda was in her office reviewing their stock portfolio. George was upstairs cleaning up the "dust-gathering boxes of junk." And Sadie was quickly learning she could do no wrong, and taking every advantage of that fact. In fact, she was lying on the carpet on her back, casually catching treats being carefully tossed by her mistress.

George came downstairs and hurried into the office holding out a very dirty and timeworn black leather book labeled Diary. "You won't believe this, Baby. I've been perusing Uncle Hiram's diary. Never knew he kept one. He died thirty years ago."

"Hiram, eh. Your mother's unmarried brother who left her this house, which passed to you after she died. Wasn't he the one with the chair with a single rocker? Refrigerator filled up with fruitcakes?"

"And there's more in here," George said as he waved the diary. His eyes opened like full moons. "He says he believes living beings can pass on their characteristics and propensity to do good or evil to their offspring."

"Now *that* is weird."

"Uncle Hiram had a cat. A very kind and good-hearted cat."

"And?"

"Her name was Sadie."

At this, the cat rolled over, stood, and emitted a loud purr.

WHERE JACK?

Wallace Graham

"We can't find it," Dad said. He tapped his right foot several times and huffed. "You're sure that it's in the house?"

Sitting in her chair, Grandma grabbed her cane. "I haven't laid eyes on that old thing since I made him stop smoking." She bounced its rubber foot between her feet.

"Easy. No need to get up. We'll find it…eventually."

Grandma slumped into her chair and scowled. They never got along. Grandpa and she told stories about fairies like they did with Mom. They taught me all the rituals. Dad scoffed at the stories "They're fantasy and shouldn't be filling your head with nonsense." I stood in the doorframe between the living room and kitchen under a mounted horseshoe. Their home was empty without Grandpa.

He looked right at me. "Any luck in the garage?"

"No, sir," I groaned. "It's not here. I want to go home."

"We can't leave without that pipe and tobacco box. Mom sent us here to get it. It was your grandfather's favorite."

"She should have come herself," Grandma said, pouting her lip.

"She can't. With the pandemic, the hospital's short staffed." He strode to the fireplace, eyed an empty saucer with a funny look, and shifted his eyes to Grandma. He thrummed his fingers on the fireplace mantle as he scanned the room. He locked his eyes on the attic drop-down door.

"Maybe it's up there?" Dad said and walked underneath to study it. "How do you open it? There's no string."

"It can't be up there. Haven't opened it in years," Grandma said.

"Well, it's the last place to look. Besides, it's been years since you've seen it, right?" He looked at me and pointed. "Son, go to the garage and get a crowbar or claw hammer."

I hung my head and drooped my shoulders. "Do I have to? I'm hungry."

"Stop moping and go. I'll get you something once we leave."

I plodded through the kitchen.

"Grab a piece of cake. There's plenty," Grandma called.

Cake! I thought and slung open the refrigerator door.

The sweet lemon smell energized me. I bounced and clapped in an unrehearsed jig. It beckoned, yellow cake with honey lemon frosting. Several missing pieces left a gap for easy nabbing. I snatched a piece and stuffed it into my mouth. Swallowing, I took a second piece before closing the refrigerator.

"Don't take all day. Hurry up," Dad said.

I huffed and shuffled out the kitchen door. In the garage, dirt coated everything. I held my cake close. I bobbed and weaved my head around all the obstacles and objects not touching a thing…except my cake. At the back workbench, I spotted a hammer. "It's all dirty," I said.

After a bite, I secured my cake in one hand. With pointer finger and thumb, I lifted the hammer from the bottom of the handle. At a slow pace, I marched back to Dad without dropping it or my cake.

He pinched his eyebrows and frowned as I entered. Yanking on a bent coat hanger, he lowered the attic door. "Don't look at me like that. You took too long." He unfolded the stairs and planted them on the floor. "Now, up you go."

"I don't want to. I'm tired."

"Why don't you sit down? I'll go up and get it." Grandma strained to rise from her chair.

"No. He's eight years old and capable." He looked at me and exhaled through his nose. "He's smaller and more agile than either of us. Now, put down that hammer and go." He pointed into the attic. I laid the hammer on the ground next to my feet. "Not there. In the kitchen."

I groaned and snatched the hammer from the floor. Stomping into the kitchen, I plopped the hammer on the table. I returned, moaning. Grandma, now, frowned at me but remained quiet.

"That pipe won't find itself," Dad said and stepped aside.

Securing my cake, I scurried into the attic. The musty old smell mixed with mild body odor greeted me. Wooden planks lined a path down the center. I stooped walking toward the back and still bumped my head. Rubbing my head after the second bump, a yellow toy shined from the faded shadows. It poked out of a box. Kneeling next to the box, I dug with my free hand.

Wow! Look at all the stuff, I thought and pulled out a yellow toy train. Wrinkling my nose, I set aside several dolls. Wooden blocks layered the bottom of the box. I removed three.

"You find it?" Dad asked.

"No, not yet."

"Keep looking. It must be up there."

Leaving the toys out, I scooted further into the attic. At the back, a pile of clutter and clothes formed a nest. *Grandpa's overalls*, I recognized. Pulling out the overalls, I found one of his t-shirts, several tools, sandpaper, and socks. On the far side, I stumbled onto his pipe and tobacco box.

"Found it," I said.

"Good. Bring it down. I'll meet you at the base of the stairs."

I reached with my free hand but couldn't grasp the box. I eyed my cake.

I can't set it down. It'll get dirty. I lifted it to my mouth while I supported the box with my other hand. *It's crumbling. I can't eat it either.*

I fumbled the box. The pipe clattered across the planks. I huffed and crawled to the pipe. I grabbed the fat part and heard a growl rise in pitch. Turning to the source, a pair of eyes shimmered in the dark like cats' eyes. I gasped and dropped to my butt.

A scream bellowed from the shadows. I matched the scream as a wrinkled hairy hand pinned my head to the ground. Body odor wafted from it and stifled my screams. It pressed and dug fingers into my temple and cheek. A thumb dug under my chin and tilted my head back. I couldn't see it. With its bodyweight on my stomach, I cowered underneath. With a free hand, it pried the pipe from mine.

"Mine. No take," it said in a shrill voice. It shook me. I howled with sobs. "You bad. You take."

Dad poked his head into the attic. "Son, you okay?"

I extended a hand. "Daddy?"

His eyes widened as he shrieked. The thing on me screamed, too. Leaping off, it grabbed a wooden block and hurled it at my dad. The block nailed him in the center of his forehead. He tumbled off the stairs and went silent.

Curling against a wooden support and dust covered shoe boxes, I balled, "No!" Splinters dug into my back as I pushed past. Stopped by boxes full of clothes, I covered my head.

With his back to me, a little wrinkled hairy man heaved. He looked over his shoulder. He bounced around. His deep brown face scowled. Bulbous lips protruded beyond sagging cheeks. Clean rags of different dark colors draped from his body. They swayed as he stomped closer.

"Who you? You bad. Why take?" he asked, wagging the pipe in my face.

I screeched, kicked, and threw my cake. I missed, but his eyes caught the cake. He traced its arc behind a stack of quilts. His wide eyes bounced from the cake and to me. Dropping the pipe, he smacked his lips.

"O-o-o, cake," he cheered and dove behind the quilts.

I scrambled to my knees, snatched the pipe, and bear crawled to the attic door. Lowering my legs onto the stairs, the springs squeaked. The gobbling sounds behind the quilts stopped. His head peered over them. He roared and barreled through them. I dropped to the ground where my dad laid unconscious.

The brown person yelled through the opening. "Mine. You bad. You take. Give back." He disappeared into the attic, and the sounds of crashing and banging thundered overhead. Dropping the pipe, I shook my dad until a glass bowl soared out of the attic. It shattered near my leg. I scurried behind Grandma.

"Grandma," I begged. "Call 9-1-1."

"I'm so sorry, Roger," she said between sniffles.

"That's not Dad's name."

"He's lived with us for years. One of the family." She pulled a handkerchief from her pocket and wiped her eyes. More bellowing and clamoring sounded from the attic.

"Who? The little man?"

"He's a brownie. He loved your grandpa very much. When your mom left, they became best friends. We weren't alone anymore." She burst into tears.

"What do we do? Dad's hurt. I can't, not by myself," I asked with gentle shakes of her arm. She said nothing. She only cried.

I sat, tucked next to Grandma, and stared at my dad. I listened to Roger scream, "Give back. You trick. Mine. Pipe mine."

My stomach tightened. *I feel sick,* I thought. *I don't want to throw up. I just had cake.*

"The cake!" I blurted. I inhaled through my nose and tightened my lips to stop trembling.

Staying low, I followed the wall into the kitchen and whisked the cake pan from the refrigerator. I shuffled into the living room shielding my head with the pan. Several quilts, pants, and socks bombarded my ascent into the attic.

"Stop," I shouted, halfway up the stairs. "You'll ruin the cake."

Grandma snapped out of her sobbing fit. "Jack, don't. It's not safe."

Too late. Roger stopped and flitted his eyes between the cake and me. Hearing Grandma broke his ranting. "Where Jack? No Jack. Want Jack."

I backed against the attic's opening edge. "I'm Jack," I said, shielding myself with the cake pan. The yellow cake dumped into a pile between us.

He snarled. "You lie. You cheat. You take." He stomped and pounded his fists in the air repeating. "Lie." His curled hair changed into straight gray fur. His ears pointed and grew tufts like a lynx. "Cheat." His saggy cheeks and protruding lips formed into the snout of a rat exposing large front teeth. "Take." His rags tightened against his body. Claws emerged on his hands and feet. "Where Jack?" Quills extended from the large tuft of hair on his head. A tail whipped and knocked through stacks of boxes. He bounded forward. Stopping at the cake, he bellowed, "No Jack!"

I quivered behind the cake pan. Peeking over it, I spotted tears running down his face. *Him too?* Tears ran down my cheeks. I lowered the cake pan. In my face, he roared. I flinched and raised the pan. From behind the pan, I asked, "You miss Grandpa? I miss him, too."

Roger roared into the pan but choked on his sobs. I dropped the cake pan and threw my arms around his head without thinking. He gasped and pulled back. His struggle eased. We held each other and cried as he returned to normal.

"We always played in the garage," I said.

He separated and said through blubbering, "Make toys. Fix home."

Wiping away tears, I jumped. Grandma placed the pipe in my dangling hand with a soft smile. I took it.

"Sorry," I said and held it to Roger.

"Mine," he said, snatching it to his chest. He scooted several steps and glanced. Scooping a glob of cake, he stuck it in my face. "Cake?"

I nodded and accepted with open hands. He scurried deep into the attic. Grandma guided me down the stairs. At the sight of Dad, I bounded next to him.

"It's alright. I called the paramedics," Grandma said.

Dad stirred and opened his eyes. Confused, he studied me. "What happened?"

"You missed a step, Harold," Grandma said. He placed a hand on the back of his head. "Don't get up. They said to stay put."

He grunted and studied my face a little harder. "Hey, it's alright. I'll be fine. Your old man's got a hard head."

Huh? I thought. I turned to Grandma, who giggled.

"Your eyes are red from crying." She patted the back of my head. "Why don't we put out a saucer of cream? That'll make everything better."

I smiled. "Then, I can come back, and maybe stay the night?"

"We'll see, dear child."

We waited for the paramedics as she told stories about Roger. Dad lay against the floor and groaned at every word.

ONE MAN'S TRASH

Judy Creekmore

Uncle John Schnokit was a hoarder. The self-proclaimed savior of no-longer appreciated artifacts had surrounded himself with items rescued from inattentive neighbors in addition to his own detritus. I never knew Mother's uncle, and the stories she told of his decline had become vague memories of no importance—until I became his heir.

I learned from his lawyer that John's wife Mary had been declared dead five years earlier, and now with John's death in Santa Barbara, California, I was the last of the Allerton-Schnokit line. Also, with full disclosure, Lawyer said that John had accumulated enough "treasures" in his 1920s Spanish Colonial Revival home, and its surrounding four acres, to become a neighborhood hazard. "That does not make me want to hop on a plane to come settle his estate," I said.

"But things are better there now," Lawyer hastened to add. "John was recently featured on a television program that explicitly shows people in danger of losing their homes and endangering their own health because of this unfortunate mental illness." He went on to tell me where I could stream John's episode of the television show.

The opening shot was of a man who looked vaguely like my mother. He was well-groomed and well-spoken, so it was a shock when the camera panned out to include his backdrop of mountains of junk. John, tears in his eyes, looked heavenward as he told the program's "Obsessive Hoarding Counselor" that his wife left him twelve years earlier and the hoarding tendencies that Mary had kept at bay went unfettered. The counselor offered words of guidance and encouragement. Soon a clean-up crew of neighbors and professionals—all wearing hazmat suits—went to work. John pulled on rubber gloves. There were shots of him placing items he deemed salvageable onto the weed-choked patio. Other scenes caught each flinch as volunteers took sledgehammers to wood and drywall covered with mold and rotten from rat droppings and urine. Huge dumpster trucks hauled away seven tons of trash. Gallons of bug spray and bleach subdued undesirable life forms.

At the end of the episode, neighbors paraded the street carrying donations of used furniture to replace the moldy piles that had once been fine antiques. In the closing minutes John, clearly a broken man, clung to a frame containing Mary's photo. "It smells much cleaner now," he mumbled, and the counselor and clean-up crew surrounding him beamed. John promised the hoarding specialist that he would continue counseling and never hoard again. And he didn't. The counselor told viewers that John had died before the episode aired.

When I asked about John's death, Lawyer said that my uncle's already inflamed lungs were overcome by fumes from residual disinfectant and insecticide in his newly germ-free home.

I said I couldn't possibly leave my home in Tennessee, that I had dogs, Ipsy and Miss Lulu, to care for and that my idea of world travel was to spend a single night away from home—preferably at the Peabody Hotel in Memphis.

"John's will states that you must visit the house and remove items of Schnokit family history before deciding to sell it," he countered.

"Interstate travel is not on my bucket list."

"Without your cooperation the estate could be tied up for years to come," Lawyer said. "The estate is worth in excess of thirty million dollars and my firm gets its money however you decide," his voice trailed off.

Funds to make sizable charitable donations made me consider air travel; and lawyers continuing to bill the estate while its fate was being decided made sleeping in a strange bed more acceptable. "I'll come."

ഗ

A week later, Lawyer met me at the house where he handed over the keys, a pair of coveralls, a box of face masks, and a list of contacts. "I've put a box lunch, various soft drinks and water in the refrigerator for you. Call my secretary if you need anything," he said with one foot out the door.

Unhappy about being dumped, I sputtered indecipherable words at his vanishing Mercedes until it disappeared around a corner. I shook the ring of keys at him and almost went to my rental car. But, "Ipsy and Ms. Lulu's Home for Abandoned Dogs" had already taken shape in my mind.

I found out that all the trash had been removed from the main floor, and the rooms held odd pieces of shabby furniture. A basic refrigerator, and a coffee maker with a variety of coffee blends, appeared new. Finally, only the large basement and attic were left for my inspection. I hesitated before testing the light cord that dangled over the first step down. Once pulled, a small portion of uncluttered basement appeared along with the usual heating, ventilating and air conditioning equipment. A dozen neatly stacked boxes marked "Mary's Things" were clean and almost dust-free. With one room left, I was optimistic.

The door to the walk-in attic required keys for three locks that I considered overkill for a room full of desiccated silverfish that had fed off crumbling cardboard boxes. Dust, hoary on every surface, went up my nose and into my eyes. An antique Louis Vuitton canvas steamer trunk was tucked away in a corner, so I went back downstairs for the pink Dyson G-Force cleaner I'd seen in the laundry room. After pulling on the coveralls, I vacuumed the silverfish bodies off the chest and discovered it was full of Allerton-Schnokit family memorabilia. I left it in place for a thorough cleaning and sorting. The attic also held dozens of large trash bags that I had to open to determine if they were indeed filled with the debris from John's life and not important historical documents.

The deeper into the mound I went, the older, more brittle the plastic. I almost tossed the last bag without peeking, but it was heavy and broke open. The top layers were old designer clothes, musty and moth-eaten from their long confinement, and leather shoes and purses with powdered mold that wafted away when I touched it. I almost retied the bag, but maybe there was something of Mary's in one of the purses? The powder blue leather Prada handbag was empty. The black Bottega Veneta leather tote held a flattened quart-sized milk jug. *Why would anyone put trash in a nice bag?* Freeing the jug, a slight noise invited me to find its source. A sunray coming through the attic window highlighted a faint shadow in the semi-opaque container. I sat back on my heels. "That is definitely a steak knife." A wad of fabric shifted with the knife as I turned the jug and looked at it from different angles. Mom had told me the story of Uncle John and Aunt Mary several times, and I listened with only slight interest. Now dead for three years, she was probably looking down on me with a nod and a smirk, "I tried to tell you."

Here's what I pieced together from memory: Twelve years earlier, the family scandal had been that Aunt Mary had left Uncle John. To hear him tell it, she had filled a suitcase, called a taxi, and left a note saying she'd had enough of his trashy ways and would visit her estranged sister in Colorado until she decided what to do. Months later, a concerned neighbor who had received a brief text saying, "Visiting my sister for a while," alerted police. When Mary's sister said Mary had not been there, John told police his wife had taken $20,000 from their joint checking account when she left. Since the sister said she couldn't tell if the writing and signatures were Mary's, there was no proof otherwise. John, who willingly went in for questioning, had the note, the withdrawal receipt, and a charge statement showing the one-way train ticket purchase. Local law enforcement had not been able to gather enough evidence for a search warrant despite the neighbor's insistence that Mary would surely have contacted someone in their Bridge Club.

Now, in the attic, I shook the jug and rust-red flakes turned to dust as they fell from the knife blade and handle. I set the jug aside and pulled the fragile bag from around the clothes. About a week's worth of what had been expensive clothing, toiletries and prescription medication seemed to have been dumped into the bag, without care for future use. *Like a man packing away things he never expected to be seen again.*

I was tired and wanted someplace more comfortable to think. My recliner was thousands of miles away, so I stripped off my dusty coverall and drove to the luxurious hotel suite Lawyer had reserved for me. That night, after a quick call home to talk to Ipsy and Ms. Lulu, I settled into the comfy bed and plump pillows. With each doze came a new variable and scenario that demanded consideration.

The next morning I ate a quick breakfast in the hotel restaurant and was soon back in the attic of John's house. I set a new box of trash bags on the floor and pulled on a fresh pair of gloves. The clothes and toiletries from the day before went into a bag that I tied off and set aside. During the next couple of hours while I sorted through things in the trunk, the milk jug, propped on a windowsill, teased me as the light outside shifted bright, then overcast. *Now you see a knife. Now you don't. That is definitely a bloody cloth. Well, maybe not.*

I picked up the jug and considered all I'd thought about the night before. *Should I call the police and tell them I found a missing piece of a twelve-year-old puzzle?* John was dead. I shook the jug. *Mary is probably dead.* If I turned the knife over to the police, would they open an investigation? How would that affect settling the estate?

After making a couple of quick phone calls, my filthy coveralls went into a bag, along with used tissues, and food containers from yesterday's lunch, followed by the jug and its contents. I placed my two bags of trash among the others and went downstairs. While I waited, one last walk through the house fed my imagination as I tried to guess how life might have played-out for John and Mary. Regardless, money from the sale of their home could benefit many battered women, food banks, and dogs.

A short burst of classical music filled the house announcing the arrival of a leather-skinned, taciturn man who'd come to pick up the trash I'd called about. He filled the back of his pickup truck and said his wife would be along the next day to clean the house and pack the Schnokit memorabilia for shipping to Tennessee. While he was busy, I called the realtor that Lawyer had supplied and told her we would discuss a contract once the memorabilia reached my home in Tennessee. There was just enough time to drop off the keys for Lawyer and drive to the airport for my flight home.

That was a few years ago. I've heard nothing more about Mary's disappearance. The locked trunk sits in my attic and contains a single safe deposit box key and an envelope of introduction and instructions. I am the last Allerton-Schnokit, but there are many Allerton descendants who will have to decide what to do with the authenticated 400 year-old draft of the "Agreement Between the Settlers of New Plymouth," and other historical documents and artifacts currently stored in a security vault. John's legacy to me was property worth $42 million. There is now a shelter for battered women that bears Mary's name and a food bank named for John.

TRAINS IN THE ATTIC

Nick Nixon

When I was a kid, a lot of little boys had Lionel Electric Train Sets. I got mine one Christmas. There was an engine, a coal car, a couple of freight cars, a passenger car and a red caboose. *All* trains had red cabooses back then. One of the houses we lived in, as I was growing up, had a small, floored attic with a built-in work bench against one wall. My father attached my train tracks to a piece of thin plywood and set that on top of the work bench. It was the perfect height. I could stand or sit on a stool and play with it.

My older sister, Dale, made me a tunnel out of a round Quaker Oats box. They still sell Quaker Oats in those tall, round boxes. She cut the top and bottom off and then made an incision right down the middle. Spread it a little and voila…instant train tunnel. But she wasn't through. She painted it to look like it was made of bricks. Yep, she was quite a good painter, even though she was only a teenager. She became quite the oil painter later in her life.

I also had little cowboys and Indians, some horses and even a few cows I played with. Add a few little cars and trucks and I had the beginnings of scenery. Scenery? Hmmm…I needed some scenery. How 'bout some hills and maybe even a mountain. I couldn't very well bring grass up there, but I did think about it…*yeah like that would pass inspection by my mother.* How 'bout some rocks and gravel? Our driveway had lots of gravel. I thought I remembered seeing some big rocks in that vacant lot just down the street all the kids liked to play in. A couple of those would make good mountains.

Trees…I needed trees. I saw some weeds that kinda looked like little trees. Great idea. Okay, so they wouldn't live very long, but that was okay. There were plenty of 'em in the yard.

When I finally had collected all the stuff I thought I needed and carefully arranged it properly, everything looked pretty good.

Uh...wait a minute, something was missing. It didn't have any buildings. I knew where I could get one building. My toy box was an old wooden tool chest at the foot of my bed. It was about the size of a cedar chest, but a whole lot more rustic...*befitting a little boy's bedroom.* I rummaged around in it till I found an old Log Cabin Syrup can that my mother had thrown in the trash. It looked just like a log cabin. It was a little out of scale, but that was okay.

I realized I could make some other buildings out of cardboard and tape. I didn't have any paint and I wasn't allowed to touch my sister's stuff, so I glued paper to the little cardboard buildings and colored 'em with crayons. I thought everything looked pretty good. Too bad I didn't have a camera back then. I would like to have picture of all that now.

My friend, Richard Bowen, had a Lionel Electric Train set too, but he had multiple engines, more cars and a lot more track. His parents had sprung for other cool train accessories too. One of his engines even pumped out smoke from the smokestack and made the sound of a whistle. When he came to our house, he would bring some of his train stuff.

My mother and I would ride the bus downtown every Saturday so she could do some shopping. Back in those days all the big department stores in Memphis were downtown on Main Street, including Goldsmith's, Lowenstein's, Gerber's, Black & White Store (which later became Shainbergs), Bry's, Bond's, Julius Lewis and lots of other smaller shops. My favorite store was Kress' 5 & 10 Cent Store. The biggest dime store in town! It even had multiple floors, and the toy department was in the basement, and it was *enormous.* She would always buy me a new toy there...if I was being a good boy. It was located across the street from Court Square, where we could buy treats and feed them to the squirrels and pigeons.

Santa Claus was always there at Christmas in a big, elaborate display in front of Court Square with snow, lights and a long ramp that led up to Santa and his elves in front of his make-believe workshop. He had a microphone with speakers that could be heard up and down Main Street. I guess I got my first big laugh from a crowd there. Santa always asked the boys and girls if they had been good all year, before he would ask them what they wanted for Christmas and give them a little gift. My mother told me to tell him, "So-so," when he asked me. That's what I said, and the crowd erupted with laughter. I kinda liked that and I've been making people laugh ever since.

When I was in junior high school, I discovered the Hobby Shop, located in an alley right next to Kress. Wow, it was great! If I had known about it when I was a little kid and if I had money to spend back then, our attic probably would not have been big enough for all the trains, tracks and accessories I would have bought. But by this time, I was into building car, airplane and ship model kits. The Hobby Shop had tons of these, plus everything else you can imagine, including little bottles of model paint, brushes and Dupont Duco Cement in little tubes. It was quite small and always crowded. Later on, in the 1960s, when all the big department stores and most of the smaller stores left downtown, the Hobby Shop moved out east to a much larger location. Same ownership, but the magic of that little shop in the alley was gone.

I miss what Main Street and downtown used to be back in the 1940s, '50s and part of the '60s. There were stores and shops all up and down Main Street. And several movie theatres: the Warner Theatre, the Malco (now the Orpheum), the Strand, and Lowe's State. Lowe's Palace was just off Main on Union. The Warner Theatre was actually built over an alley. The ticket office and marble entrance were on Main Street, but we had to climb wide marble steps to a landing, then more steps to the main lobby where the concession stand was. There were huge floor to ceiling mirrors and brass railings on either side of these steps.

The lobby was literally over a functional alley that big trucks could drive through. When you walked into the actual theatre, you were in the balcony level. You had to walk down steps to the main floor. Everything beyond the concession stand of the Warner Theatre was located between the alley and Second Street. The screen, stage and anything else behind the screen backed up to Second Street.

Downtown Memphis had several very nice hotels: the Peabody, the Chisca, the Gayoso and the William Lynn were great hotels with fine restaurants. And there were other restaurants in the downtown area. You could easily make a day and a night of it in downtown in those days. There were also two train stations in downtown Memphis, Central Station, located on Main Street, which is still operating, and Memphis Union Station, which sadly is gone.

Did you think I wasn't going to mention trains again? Say, have you ever ridden The City of New Orleans?

CLARA'S BIBLE

Sharilynn Hunt

Trudy opened the attic door and yelled. "Nana, are you up there?" With a muffled response from her grandmother, she bounded the stairs like any fourteen-year-old.

Dusty boxes stacked on one another crowded her vision. "I don't remember this space being so small and crowded. I can't see you," Trudy said.

"Over here." Nana waved from the back.

Trudy saw a partial hand and stepped around the maze of old furniture and boxes. "What are you doing?"

"Since I'm moving to smaller quarters, I need to sort through this attic. This cedar chest belonged to my grandmother Adele; I inherited it when my mother died. But, I haven't looked inside for a long time."

Nana sat on a windowsill. "Here, sit down. I want to show you something." Trudy scooted next to her grandmother, looking at the big book in her lap.

Opening the metal clip, Nana said, "This Bible belonged to my great-grandmother Clara, my grandfather's mother. She lived in Philadelphia in the 1880s."

"This is a Bible? It's huge! It reminds me of a book I once saw in a museum. I'm sure the brown and gold cover with *The Holy Bible* engraved on it was once pretty. But I think it's ugly now. I can't imagine anyone using this for Bible reading or taking it to church."

Nana laughed. "No one used this for church. People would display these large Bibles on a table to record their family's genealogy. Look at the handwritten inscription on the front."

To Clara
presented by her Father and Brothers
Christmas 1883

Trudy reached for the heavy book and set it in her lap. The pages fluttered open. "It sure smells musty."

"Be careful. It's so fragile that the fat spine has lost its glue from the paper and may fall apart," Nana stated.

Two heads skimmed through the numerous references, the old English titles, the pictures, maps, and drawings of each disciple. Nana's finger rolled down the lists of the family's births, deaths, and marriages from previous generations.

"Clara received this one hundred and thirty-nine years ago. Here are the names of her four children, with Grandpa Eugene being the youngest. Then she lists his five children; my mother was the last child."

"Nana, look at her beautiful cursive writing of all the names. They don't teach cursive in school anymore."

After flipping back to the title page, Nana noticed the publisher, A.J. Holman Company. "How interesting this company was in Philadelphia, and they still publish Bibles today."

Trudy tucked her feet under her. "Do you know anything more about Clara?"

"Well, I only know bits and pieces from my mother. Clara was a petite, pretty woman who always dressed in the latest fashion. Her parents moved from England and were active in the Episcopal Church in Philadelphia.

"Clara's family started a liquor company in the 1880s, and I guess they were successful and wealthy from it. Eugene, her son, had the reputation of being a ladies' man and dated many society girls in the city before he moved to Chicago as the main typesetter for the Chicago Tribune."

"So how did he meet your Grandma Adele? Was she rich too?"

"No, she grew up on a farm in middle Pennsylvania. Originally from Germany, her people were called Pennsylvania Dutch. After her mother died when she was eight, two older brothers went to live with neighbors, and she had to do all the cooking and cleaning for her father and younger brothers. When she was fourteen, she ran away to Pittsburg and lived in a boarding house until she got married."

"Gosh, that's my age. I can't imagine living alone," Trudy frowned.

"Well, times were different. Young girls raised on the farms often moved to the cities for jobs, but she worked hard for a living," Nana said.

She could picture a young Adele locking the door to her boarding room and hurrying the few blocks to the hotel every morning. "Would there be sheets and towels to mend today," Adele wondered, "or will I have to clean the rooms? I barely make ends meet, even with sewing new dresses for some girls at the boarding house and selling ribbons at the dry goods store on Saturdays.

"But every day, I'm happy on my own, not under the roof of a mean father who yelled and cussed, sometimes slapping me around. Glad he got a new wife to cook and clean for my brothers."

Adele smiled, touching the last letter from Eugene in her pocket. Six months ago, she and her friend, Sara, finally saved enough cash for a fall visit to Coney Island. Who knew she would meet the love of her life at a hot dog stand?

With Eugene and his friend, the four of them laughed all day while riding the rides and large carousel and eating at various food stands along the boardwalk. Eugene's good looks, big brown eyes, and charming personality captured her heart. It was the best day of her life!

Now being spring, she formulated a plan. Her cousin Alice also lived in Chicago and was very sick. If she rode the train one weekend in June to visit Alice, she could also see Eugene.

A few weeks later, Adele stepped off the Chicago train and saw a handsome man dressed in his navy suit and wearing a big grin. Two days later, she married Eugene at the courthouse on June 3, 1908. He telegraphed his mother the news, and Adele's landlord agreed to send her meager belongings in the small cedar chest by the Chicago train.

"So, when did Grandma Adele meet Clara?" Trudy asked.

"I'm not sure, but after each child arrived, Clara visited them. I heard the two never got along, so Eugene traveled to Philadelphia alone each year to visit his family. Maybe the old-fashioned traditional woman resented her son's marriage to a working-class girl,"

"Did your grandparents fight a lot?" Trudy asked.

"Yes. There was a lot of contention in the house and one infamous visit with Clara too," Nana said.

Eugene walked into the kitchen and announced to the family, "I've invited my mother to visit us before the summer is over to see the kids."

Adele swirled around and shouted. "That woman is not staying again in this house, always bragging about her new furniture and the latest fashions. If she comes, we'll leave!"

"Can't you be nice? After all, it's been a few years since she's been here."

"When your mother visits, she wears fine clothing, high heels, and stylish hats with French rose perfume around her neck. She's not fooling me, bringing each grandchild a new outfit, making my homemade ones look plain. It's hard keeping five kids clothed on our budget," Adele's voice dripped with sarcasm.

When Clara got out of the cab, Adele met her on the steps, "You sit on the porch until Eugene comes home. Since I'm cooking dinner, I'll send the girls out to entertain you."

Clara sat down with a huff on the front rocker glaring at Adele. The youngest three girls bounced out the door with hugs and kisses and sat on the stoop. They entertained their grandmother by talking nonstop about all their school activities until Eugene walked up the sidewalk.

True to her word, after dinner, a neighbor's son stuck his head in the front door, "Are you ready, Ms. Adele?" Eugene looked puzzled.

"Yes, we're ready," said the young mother as she herded all the kids with suitcases out the door. They drove to a river cabin fifty miles away, leaving a bewildered mother-in-law and one red-faced husband who stared at a table full of dirty dishes.

A few nights later, Adele shook the sleeping Clara at eleven o'clock. "Get dressed and wait downstairs for the morning cab to take you back to the train station. Eugene will make you some coffee and wait with you," Adele spoke loudly.

A tearful grandmother and son sat until dawn until she left for the station. No one ever saw Grandma Clara again.

"Gosh, how horrible," Trudy said.

"Yes. You know, rudeness and anger can bring bitterness into the home. Then the family went through some hard times."

After the stock market crashed in 1929, Eugene, bedridden with heart issues, could barely walk, much less go to work before Christmas. Adele rubbed and wrapped his swollen legs daily, but fear grabbed and held on during her nightly prayers. In February 1930, Eugene took his last breath at forty-nine, and the young family spiraled into financial disaster.

"Your father didn't try hard enough to live," Adele told her family.

Meals often included soups, cabbage, potatoes, and dumplings. Hope rose one Friday when the mail came with a life insurance check of $2,000. Dancing around the room, the younger girls laughed with joy.

Adele told her son, "Go straight to the bank and deposit this." She never guessed the bank would freeze all assets and close its doors on Monday. Years later, Adele received ten cents on the dollar.

"They lost all their money?" Trudy raised her eyebrows.

"Yes. Adele rented out the larger bedroom and sewed for many families. My aunt finished her teaching degree to support the family, and another uncle and aunt dropped out of high school to work. The family pulled together and made it through the Great Depression too."

Trudy thumbed through the Bible pages. "Look, two pages are stuck together with some paper inside."

"Honey, be careful. The binding is so fragile that the fat spine has lost its glue from the paper, and I'm afraid it will fall apart."

Carefully they peeled the pages away and read the faded ink.

January 1, 1930

Dear Son,

Happy New Year! I hope this note finds you in better health. I'm worried about your heart condition and have been praying for you.

Adele and I have never gotten along, but she hurt me deeply on my last visit. I've sought forgiveness from God for my resentment toward her. Please forgive me too. Hopefully, 1930 will be a better and more peaceful year for all of us.

Since I left you my treasured Bible, Eugene, I pray the words of God will give you strength and grace during these dark days. May He enlighten you to follow the path of faith, hope, and love to the Cross of Calvary.

I've enclosed some money to help with your expenses.

Much love, Mother

"Trudy, Clara wrote this note one month before Eugene died, and I wonder if anyone else ever read it. I heard she died from a stroke a few weeks later, so the grandmothers probably never found peace between them. Offenses can be never-ending, just like in these two."

Trudy turned to the empty cardboard frames in the back made for family pictures. "Gosh, I wish we had a picture of Clara. Can we put a picture of us in a frame for future generations?"

Looking at the top of the cardboard, Trudy saw a tiny bulge. Squeezed between the hardened paper were two fifty-dollar bills. "Nana, this must be Clara's money! I bet Grandpa Eugene hid it before he died, and no one ever found it."

"They sure could have used this money, but I'm surprised this Bible lasted in the care of a daughter-in-law who never liked Clara," Nana replied.

Trudy closed the book and placed it inside the chest.

"Nana, what are you going to do with the money?"

"I was thinking. Maybe we should donate it. The downtown Episcopal church recently opened a women's shelter for mothers who need financial help. I believe this money could symbolize reconciliation and peace between my two grandmothers."

"Trudy nodded her head. "I like that. And Nana, can I inherit the Bible someday?"

"Absolutely. I'm sure Grandma Clara would be pleased."

Editor's note: Credited to twelfth century troubadours, a sestina is an intricate thirty-nine line poem following a strict pattern. It features the repetition of end-words in six stanzas, culminating in a three-line concluding stanza.

TRIO DI SESTINA: JOURNEY OF MEMORIES

John Burgette

Canto I

He steadied himself on his walking cane as he pulled out a pair of blue
jeans. Obviously too small for him, he guessed they were from when he was fourteen. He remembered the jeans he'd wear, while sitting back in a lawn chair with a can
of pop — after mowing the grass with a push mower. They were faded and torn because
they were worn for years; as long as they would last. It seemed the brass
rivets were about all that kept the material together. Then, he saw the rod and reel.

In a near corner, there was his mud-stained rod and reel.
Immediately, he remembered a morning under a sky, so blue
and with fluffy clouds. In his small boat, he would bait the brass
barbed hook, and throw the line into the water. Waiting for
the cork to bobble, he'd stare across the waters, which would often cause
him to miss the nibble; so, he'd keep trying as long as he had worms in an old tin can.

Beyond a pile of colorful periodicals, he saw the rusty gasoline can,
which had been in the trunk of his first automobile. It didn't move real
fast, and it often had flats, but it was his first, and so, one of his favorite cars.
It had four doors (three worked), a good radio, and it was his favorite color — blue.
Constantly in need of repair, it didn't last, due to wear — maybe four
months, but he was able to trade it in for an old truck; with chrome so rusted, it looked like brass.

Within a small, torn case, he found a flute made of brass.
Quickly, he put it together and blew into the mouthpiece, but he could
not make a sound, except the whistling of air. He had played it for
high school band. He was always in the last chair because he wasn't really
a good player. They practiced classical music & marches, but he wanted to perform the blues.
Slowly, he placed the instrument back into its case when he noticed the miniature cars.

Inside a huge cardboard box was a pile of toy cars —
trucks & autos made of plastic, and some built from metal; with axles made of brass
or steel. Not a surprise — one of his favorite cars was a blue
race car. He would roll its wheels backwards to wind a spring and point it at a trash can
laying on its side from across the kitchen, and then — real
slowly — he'd release it, and it would speed across the floor in five seconds, maybe four.

Beyond the box of toy automobiles, he counted four
boxes of various letters and cards he had kept because
they were all to — or from — his late wife. “Ours was a real
love,” he thought, as his eyes watered, and he grasped the brass
handle of his cane. One letter, he had sent to her from Caen
in France; its envelope, like most of them, were the color of her eyes — blue.

He rested for a few moments, while leaning on his brass topped cane,
because he realized he hadn’t found the yoga mat. He sat on top of an old trash can,
and thought, “So far, I have only found fond memories, sentiment, and a bit of blues.”

Canto II

Deeper into the room he went, and he found a green
army uniform that belonged to his father, Ed. In 1942, Ed was sent
to fight, and in 1945, he returned with several medals —
after many battles and campaigns, the allies had won
the war. His family and friends welcomed Ed and his impressive record,
but he was so much more excited because he had missed them all so.

Further on, he found a basket with needle and thread — his mother, Agnes, had loved to sew.
There were many types of yarn and thread, as well as many colors, including green,
blue, red, white, and yellow. Agnes would also use yarn to record
messages like, “Home Sweet Home.” She looked for bargains, and for one cent,
she once bought a big red pincushion. No matter the subject, every one
of her projects she did carefully — serious art, which she made with cotton and metal.

Lying on the floor, among pieces of insulation, was a crooked metal
crank, used to start an old truck — Ed’s first vehicle. Large bags of seed to sow,
Ed had hauled to various farmers, who raised corn and cotton on one
of the biggest fields in the county. In the summer, the field became a green
ocean. It was a reliable old truck, and Ed drove it for many years. Ed never sent
it more than 15 miles from home; dependable, but slow — it beat no speed records.

Sitting on a wood cabinet was an old phonograph, which was next to a box of records.
He thought about the beautiful sounds that could emerge from the scratching of a metal
needle against a slab of vinyl. Agnes would sit and listen to the music with a sense
of wonder. There was a record, in particular, that had a song on it that would make her so
sentimental. It was the song Ed played when he proposed to her; even from afar, the green
label on the disk revealed to her — of all of the records — that was her favorite one.

Next to the wood cabinet, there was a white sheet wrapped around one
large bag of young Ed’s toy marbles. Marbles were played on the sheet, and a record
of game scores were written on it in pencil. Some marbles had blue, green,
and yellow glass swirls, which circled its middle, where there was a small piece of metal.

Near the center of the sheet, was a ring where an opponent's marbles would be placed; so
Ed would shoot a large marble at the bunch and keep any, when out the circle they were sent.

On a bedside table was a purple bottle — when opened, it emitted a very sweet scent.
Ed brought it back from Europe, when he returned from the war. It was one
of her favorite keepsakes. Agnes was careful not to waste, and so,
she only applied a little of the perfume before each anniversary dinner, where the record
with her favorite song would be played. They'd take a walk, & she wouldn't let anyone meddle
in the celebration — no children nor grandchildren — just her and Ed on the ocean of green.

He'd sent himself to find a yoga mat, but so far, all he had was an ekphrastic record for
two — not one — generations of treasures mislaid, but not forgotten; not a fortune of metals,
like so many gold coins, but of lives lived, green fields, and memories remembered.

Canto III

Near the end of the room, he found — inside a small, open container — a red
scarf. It was twisted, rumbled, and crumbled so much, it resembled a round rose.
His grandmother, Beth, had kept it, and it had originally belonged to
Beth's grandmother, Lily. Lily had carried it across the ocean from where she had been born.
"What a priceless item to not be better covered," he said, as he searched for the lid to the box.
After finding the cover, carefully, he placed it on top after taking one last look at the "ruby ball."

As he moved his foot, he noticed it had bumped against, and started rolling, a baseball.
He picked it up and saw it was signed "To: Bill" (his grandpa's name) in red
ink, but he couldn't read the signature. Bill had traveled by train to the city and had box
seat tickets to a big game. A foul ball flew very high and headed toward the rows
where Bill sat. He jumped up and caught the prize, but still had to wrestle it away from a Bears
fan. It was a memorable day for Bill, but he never, again, saw another game after 1922.

Along the back wall, he saw a long red bike: a bicycle built for two.
Beth and Bill used to ride it everywhere they could, and they had a ball
traveling around town on their bike. Both of them — standing on the pedals — would bear
their weight to see how fast they could go. People would shout at the flash of red,
"There goes Billy and Beth." Their favorite destination was the park, where between the rows
of flowers they'd ride; then, they'd stop and eat — in the basket, they always had a lunchbox.

On the floor, next to the long red bicycle, was a small metal box,
decorated in colorful porcelain. He carefully picked it up to
examine. On the side, there was a small lever, and when he pulled it, a lid rose
on the top, and a small, mechanical bird appeared; it chirped, danced, and rotated, as if on a
ball.
It sang and danced for a few more seconds, while its wings of green and red
flapped; then, it stopped and the lid closed. On the box's bottom was inscribed, "E. Baer."

Sitting in a child's little rocking chair, was Bill's old, blue teddy bear.
Bill had won the toy when he was a little boy of three — at the fair, he had hit a box
with a bean bag, and inside the box, there was a note: "You've won the bear," his mom read.
It became his favorite toy, and he took it everywhere he went. In time, its two
pasted eyes fell from its face and were replaced by brown blouse buttons. By seven, baseball
became more important to Bill, but over time, the toy's priority as a keepsake, again, rose.

Inside a large caramel-colored book, tightly closed, was a pressed rose:
to part with it, Beth could not have bore.
Bill had given Beth a bouquet of flowers at the annual spring ball,
and she kept one as part of the fond recall. The book's page framed the rose within a box
of swirled patterns Beth had drawn on a blank sheet; at the top, she wrote, "May 14, 1932."
As he carefully closed the book, he took one last look at the pressed rose, which was still red.

As he placed the book with the pasted rose on a cardboard box, he realized his search for a
yoga mat needed to bear toward a new direction. "To a sports store," he said, as he held Bill's
old baseball — signed in red — dancing away, leaving his cane for another explorer to survey.

REMNANTS OF GW

Doyne Phillips

Each trip up those attic stairs brings a bit of anxiety. Besides the usual items you see stored away, there are also remnants of our lives. Things like my youngest son Will's baseball card collection, my middle child Jason's framed Taekwondo Blackbelt diploma, and my oldest child Melanie's doll collection. As many times as we have offered these items, they just don't seem as interested in them as we are. They remain there. They, like so many other items, are remnants of our lives frozen in time.

Being a bit of a history buff, I also have a stack of newspapers that denote notable events throughout my short life span of 70 years here on earth. Wars, presidential elections, natural disasters and the like. It would have made the front page of our local, state and national papers in order to qualify as a keeper. There was one exception. The story of a personal childhood acquaintance named GW which made the front page of our county newspaper for the murder of his wife and her boyfriend.

GW was my grandfather's farm hand. He had a family of five, a wife and three children. I only knew the oldest child, a son with an imagination that would rival Walt Disney. Many mistook his imagination for being a liar. I heard it said that he told more lies than little Martha Sue that lives down the road. I never really knew who Martha Sue was, if she really existed, but I never questioned the statement.

GW was a quiet man, friendly and gentle with not only his children but with my brother and me as we were always around on the farm while they worked. Although we were just children, we found GW to be one of our favorite people to talk to. He would spend the time to explain, joke, discipline or whatever was appropriate at the time. My brother and I once found we were being disciplined by GW for throwing dirt clods at him while he was digging an irrigation ditch in front of my grandparents' home. He gave us a "talking to" that made us feel ashamed that we had done such a thing to our good friend while he was trying to help our grandfather water his crops in this hot sun. I felt terrible about it. It still bothers me to this day.

That gentle giant of a man I knew was far from the man that was described in the newspaper. As a child I didn't understand it all but remember the description of the events of that night.

Five miles in the pouring rain in the middle of the night, GW walked returning home. This was not his first trip of the night but his fourth. He left his home just after sundown and walked the five miles to confirm his suspicion. His wife Norma had been leaving the kids at home and staying out later and longer than was normal for a mother of three. GW had suspicioned she was meeting up with a fellow from the neighboring area of Steel Bridge. GW felt this had gone on long enough and he was determined to find out if his suspicions were right.

That first trip of the night took less than an hour. As GW walked, he thought about the family's need of a vehicle. He and Norma could hardly make ends meet as it was, so a vehicle was out of the question. His pay as a farm laborer and her occasional jobs cleaning houses or babysitting was not enough to save money for a car. GW walked everywhere or, if fortunate, a nearby neighbor or relative would give him and his family a ride. GW didn't seem to mind the walking himself but wished he could provide better for the family. The small children had a hard time on a long walk and it usually meant he or Norma had to carry them.

GW arrived at the home of the fellow he believed was seeing Norma. He walked to the front door and knocked. It was quiet inside so he knocked again, only this time much louder. He heard someone rustling about and soon someone came to the door. It was the fellow GW was here to see. GW, without any introduction, looked the man in the eye and asked if his wife Norma was there.

The fellow asked GW who he was. GW quickly responded he was GW Brown, husband of Norma Brown, and was there to speak to his wife. GW then asked the fellow who he was. The fellow responded he was John Bynum. GW was confused by John's confidence and boldness and thought for a minute he may have been wrong about Norma being there. Confused? Yes, but wrong, not on your life. John was quick to say I will get her.

GW's heart was breaking as Norma appeared from the back of the house. Suspicions are one thing. They may be hard to live with but the proof of her infidelity was more than he could stand. He began to cry as she approached him. As GW spoke to her, John stood behind her as if there to support Norma in her confrontation with her husband.

GW began pleading with Norma to come home with him. He reminded her how he and the kids missed her and needed her. He told her she could not leave him and the kids for this man. He told her how wrong it was to abandon the family for a fling. GW pleaded for Norma to come home and did so in front of John until he could plead no more. GW's heart was broken to the point of no shame as he asked her for her answer.

Norma began to speak, and soon GW realized she and John had been prepared for this moment. They knew they would be found out. They knew GW would confront either Norma or John or both at some point and had decided on what they would say. Their preparation had given Norma the courage to stand and deliver her farewell speech to GW. He realized Norma was leaving him and the kids for a life with John.

GW turned to leave, and as he stepped down off the porch the rain began to fall and his head began to spin with thoughts of what he would do now without his Norma. The mother of his three kids, his wife of some twelve years, his companion in the good and bad of life's situations was leaving. What would he do without her? What would the kids do without her? How would he take care of the kids alone?

GW began his five mile walk home, broken hearted, confused, searching for answers to his future. Then suddenly the hurt left and the anger took over; the anger at John for taking his Norma from him; the anger at Norma for leaving him without a wife and companion and leaving their children motherless. The harder he rain fell, the madder GW got. He realized Norma was lost and there was no getting her back. He knew what he had to do.

GW arrived home and checked on the kids. They had put themselves to bed as they would probably have to do many times now that their mother was gone. They seemed to be sleeping fine so GW began to gather his things together.

First on his list was his Daddy's old 12-gauge shotgun. His Daddy had left it to him when he died some years ago. Had it not been for this inheritance, GW probably would have never been able to afford a gun. It had been a life saver over the years for hunting game during the winter months. The garden kept them fed in the summer, but that old shotgun and GW's dead aim kept them in squirrel, rabbit and ducks in the winter.

Next were the shells. GW didn't have extra money for shells and only had a few lying around most of the time. The lack of money for shells had made GW a good shot out of necessity as it had many a farm boy in Lonoke County. Shells could not be wasted so a good aim was necessary. GW happened to have a handful and thought that should be enough.

With the shells in his pocket and the gun under his arm he left the house and started back to John's in the pouring rain, arriving within two hours of his departure. It was nearing midnight and the house was dark and quiet. John and Norma apparently had gone to bed. GW stood on John's porch and loaded the shotgun, then stepped up to the door. With one shot he blew the lock off the door and stepped inside.

GW could hear John and Norma rustling around in the bedroom in the back of the house so he headed that way. As he neared the bedroom door John came rushing out to see what the noise was. John was met with a blast from the 12 gauge hitting him in the shoulder and spinning him around. He turned from GW and ran back into the bedroom as GW fired a second shot, missing him but hitting the wall in the kitchen.

GW followed John back into the bedroom and as John stumbled across the bedroom at the foot of the bed GW shot him between the shoulder blades, bringing him down. As GW stood over him watching him die he could hear the screams of Norma hiding in the corner. He turned toward her as she ran to the bedroom door and fired a shot.

The shot missed Norma but the blast of it frightened her so she fell into the kitchen screaming and begging for her life. As GW walked toward her, Norma saw there was no mercy in him and ran toward the front room. GW fired once again, missing her but continuing to follow her for the next shot which came in the front room of the house near the front door.

GW leveled his gun and hit her high in the back near her neck. Norma collapsed on the floor dead. GW stood staring at her body, realizing he had completed the task he had set out to do and it was time to go home. He walked past her body and out the front door he had blasted open and began his last five mile walk of the night.

As GW walked home in the rain he had little thought of what was ahead for him. He had no thought of being found out, arrested, tried or sentenced for his deed. He had no thought as to the years he would serve in prison for the death of Norma and John. He had not even considered the possibility of being separated from his kids and they being placed in foster homes or an orphanage until they were grown. GW only felt the satisfaction of hurting the ones that hurt him. His rage had overcome everything else and taken control of his life from this point on.

GW was never considered to be crazy or dangerous. It's true he was never accused of being sharper than a marble, but he was not someone that meant harm to anyone until that night. The family he loved was threatened and this was the only answer he had.

GW passed away many years ago. I never heard anything about his kids. I can only hope they have good memories of their father and they know what a kind and gentle man he was. I would hate to think the only remnants of his life known to them was the account of their mother's murder.

THE DAY OF THE ATTIC'S HIDDEN TREASURES

Jan Wertz

My Day of Dread, the Day of the Attic had finally arrived. For decades I'd begged my parents to let me inherit its contents, back when I was young enough to make the many trips down the stairs necessary to haul all of the boxes stuffed with many years of accumulated, uh, 'stuff'. Mother had given me a quick decisive answer, "No! Absolutely not! You'll just throw my things away! You have no right to do that."

OK, she did have a point. I knew there were many things 'too valuable to throw out' which would never be used. Yes, I would have given as many of the 'attic stuffers' to charity as possible rather than just dumping all of the 'junk' in the trash. Either way, they would have been gone. As it was, I wasn't so young anymore, and I wasn't looking forward to the days of drudgery ahead.

After Mother passed away, Dad and I had gone through her things. Some of it had been amazing… Medications dating back decades, which had probably degraded to the point of being toxic. Small bags of untouched make-up, years old. About one thousand cookbooks filled a couple of bookcases, boxes in the attic, and bags stuffed into the hall and sewing closets. Boxes, huge boxes, full of never worn clothing bought on SALE! Mother had never met a SALE she hadn't loved. Other big boxes stuffed with knitting yarn and other such hobby supplies. Carloads of the stuff! I could hardly see to drive! Seven hundred Beanie Babies were donated to the local children's hospital, even the ones she said were 'valuable'. Oxygen tubing for use with her generator, and other such supplies, 'hidden' under her bed. Literally! Plus so much more. The church's Neighborhood Outreach blessed her for all of the donations she—via me—was providing them. Stuffed animals were used by the Outreach for Christmas gifts for children whose families New Orleans' Hurricane Katrina had displaced to this area. The list of items was long and varied. The Outreach would see it was all finally put to good use.

In among the excess items, Dad and I had found some real treasures, although we didn't always agree on just what was considered a treasure or just junk. One such collection of stuff decorated the floor in the upstairs hobby room. Assorted boxes were full of photo processor's folders of negatives and pictures from assorted vacations and family occasions spilled out onto the 1970s era shag carpet.

Another box was filled with old letter tapes; there were no markings to say who had sent what or to whom. Those 'letter tapes' had been the answer to the tedium of sitting down to hand write a letter. The same size as 8mm spools of home movie film, these were put on a reel-to-reel tape recorder, leaving the sender to fill it with a rather one-sided conversation. If a family occasion was in progress, everyone present was given an opportunity to talk to the family member or members who would receive the recording. In the movies, when a person is shown reading a letter, the audience hears the letter being read as being in the voice of the sender. With letter tapes, this wasn't a Hollywood movie illusion anymore. It was the next best thing to being there! It had always been a red-letter day to receive one of the small flat boxes in the mail!

Dad took one look at the old tapes in their jumble of individual mailer boxes in the battered cardboard box, and said, "We still have these old things? Nobody's interested in these anymore. Get rid of them." I looked at the box, and saw a treasure. The tapes did disappear, but onto the top shelf of the hall closet where they would be safely out of Dad's sight.

Once the house had been mostly cleared of Mother's things, I'd been kept busy caring for my dad. I retired from my job to give him the time needed to actually meet his needs. Caring for an elder semi-invalid required more time than I would have ever believed. Not one minute of the time he required was begrudged, but the progression of his failing health was hard to watch.

Finally, after ten years of decline, the inevitable happened. Dad passed away, leaving me with the house filled with more than just memories, including an attic full of no telling what. Mostly things not needed downstairs for every day, but too 'valuable' to get rid of. Now I was faced with emptying the attic before summer heat arrived, while also preparing the house to be sold. The dreaded Day of Reckoning had arrived. Oh, joy…

I quickly learned to be callous. I'd stuff boxes—there were lots of boxes—with non-breakables, tape them shut, wish them luck, then send each of them sliding down the steep stairs, tumbling until colliding with the back door just beyond the final step.

My cousin on Dad's side, Ed, came and spent one memorable afternoon with me. I'd told him of finding a box of old tapes, ones Dad had told me to throw out as they were just old 'junk'. This one time I'd gone against his orders, and hidden them in a well stuffed closet. With Dad gone, we both wanted to hear them.

In a moment of generosity, Ed offered to help me by hauling some of the rest of the stuff from the attic down the steep staircase. As he carried some of the things I didn't think I could just dump in a box to skid down the stairs, more items concealed by that overburden were revealed. One was a wooden box, a bit more of a square than a shoe box. I didn't remember ever seeing it before. Ed watched as I lifted the lid, revealing a few more letter tapes, an almost identical looking reel of 8mm movie film—which turned out to be something he'd been looking for—and some almost crumbling rolls of developed negatives. I admit, I had few hopes for those… Being in the attic for decades in summer heat and winter cold had damaged them badly. The temperatures in that attic were a few of the reasons I didn't expect much from the taped recordings either. What hadn't disintegrated my cousin treated with care.

Now it was time for me to clean out the house while the lawyers took care of the legalities of Dad's estate. Yes, I had been sorting and clearing out the worst of my mother's hoarding, along with the inevitable clutter. Dad had seen the boxes and bags headed to various charities, and had just shaken his head. He'd told me the house itself must be feeling relieved now that the weight of all that stuff was gone. Which didn't mean the place was actually cleaned out, only that the two of us had a bit more room to walk around. Just like the chests of drawers, the shelves in the hall closets, the attic, while a whole lot better, was still stuffed with things to be sorted through. Much of it was hauled out to be donated, sold, or put into the dumpster. A whole attic filled with things too potentially 'valuable' to be thrown out, but not wanted downstairs where the assortment would be in the way. Stuff to mostly just get rid of.

Dad had bought us a very nice reel-to-reel recorder, which would require some maintenance to repair the damage of time and neglect before it could be used to play and transcribe the old tapes to digital format. I added our collection of a few small portable recorders into that box as well. Ed took them all, the box of letter tapes, the box with the recorders, and the assortment of other treasures with him home to Birmingham. There he had his computer set up, ready to convert the audio tapes to digital format. He also had a copier which could convert the crumbling negatives to digital and reverse them to be photos rather than negatives. My cousin had his work cut out for him! It took a couple of months, but the result was worth it—to me. Considering how much time he put into the project, I was relieved when Ed told me just how much the results meant to him.

I remember the day Ed phoned me saying, "Today I heard familiar voices I haven't heard for so many years!" Some of the tapes had been made by our grandparents, Mom & Pop, in Clearwater, Florida. Some my parents had recorded going back to when we first moved to Memphis. Others had been recorded by assorted members of my extended family.

One day, when I checked my e-mail, I discovered several from Ed, each with an attached recording. I clicked on the first one and heard my grandfather announcing the day's recording by opening with a parody of the WWII news broadcasts from London. It began, "Clearwater calling! Clearwater calling! And now, over to Mom!"

My grandmother's voice asked, "Is everybody ready?" A chorus of piping children's voices eagerly answered, "Yesss!", before giving way to song. "Jesus loves me, this I know…" In that instant, listening to that long ago day, I was a little child again, just like they were, attending Mom's Wednesday afternoon neighborhood children's Bible Club. There were children's stories from the Bible, with illustrations on an easel, happy singing of the familiar songs, followed by lemonade and graham crackers. In my current home, far away in both time and place, listening to the slightly off key eager little voices, I was sitting in Mom's living room again, listening to a very familiar scene. It was as if playing the tape had given me a window into the past. I could hear everything as if it were happening in front of me, and see it all in my memory, as if via a sort of time portal. I couldn't actually join in the recorded events, nor would there ever be any changes in those events. I could watch, but not take part. Still… Some things I found in the attic dust are far more valuable to me than gold.

IF ONLY WE'D KNOWN

Michael Hicks Thompson

It's 2042. My name is Huffie Furr. I'm still living (if you want to call it that) in what used to be my grandfather's house, in Johannesburg. His name was Dr. Angus Furr. He was the primary scientist in the 2035 efforts to create oceanic cloud seeding.

Our planet was in the third year of a worldwide drought. Our lakes and rivers were gone. Creating land-based cloud seeding had been my grandfather's specialty. But without land water evaporation there weren't any clouds large enough to seed and form ice crystals to make rain. He had to find another way to make rain.

He turned to ocean clouds, where there was plenty of evaporation. But ocean clouds dropped 90 percent of their fresh water back into the sea. He slaved for years to discover a way to coax clouds over land and then deliver their life-giving pure water.

I tell you all this because I'm in my grandfather's attic. I came up here looking for photographs of his rain-making laboratory when I came across a book called *CLOUDS ABOVE*. Its cover caught my attention. I'd never seen it.

Right at the top of the book's cover was this quote: "Whoever can solve the problems of water will be worthy of two Nobel Prizes—one for science and one for peace," John F. Kennedy, 1962.

It was a powerful challenge which nobody has been able to solve. Except my grandfather who solved it *but, alas, to no avail.*

Tired and wanting to relax, I slid down the attic wall behind me. To the floor. I began to thumb through the book.

There was no signature from the author. No notes, scribbles, nothing. So, I wasn't sure if my grandfather had read it or not. The copyright was 2021, fourteen years before the worldwide drought.

Chapter 1. "Oh, my goodness" I caught myself saying. Right

away I noticed it. The story, as I read on, had some of the same situations my grandfather experienced. Like in the book, a sinister water company wanted to make sure the ocean cloud experiments failed, because rainwater would put the sewage converters out of business. The "water companies" grew like nasty weeds by converting sewage water into drinking water. One company was particularly nasty.

I've always called them sewage converters. Heck, they've been doing it since 2005, converting sewage into drinking water. And just like in the book none of the water companies wanted to see my grandfather succeed. And they tried, several times.

In the book the real hero is the grandfather's granddaughter. She's a 27-year-old prodigy. Good-looking. Nothing like me. Even her name is more erudite: Grayson Fields, Ph.D.

I kept reading. The hairs on my arm stood at attention. 'This book has too many coincidences,' I thought. 'How could someone in 2021 write an entire book about the year 2035 that came so true?'

The story even includes a broad swath of places around the globe that were suffering from lack of water, which was true now in 2042. The story in the book became more eerie and familiar as I read on.

My sore back reminded me that I'd lost two hours; only the attic fans kept me from melting. I decided to read more.

The author must've had some sort of divine intervention to write so many accurate happenings about the future. How else could he seem to know about all the things that happened 14 years before it happened?

To perform the indoor experiments, my grandfather built an indoor simulator enclosed on all sides and ceiling to create and simulate a real-life eco-system. The indoor laboratory was necessary because it was too expensive to send planes out over the ocean with each new chemical algorithm every time my grandfather changed the formula.

The simulator was a miniature land and ocean replica set atop a 36" high platform, one half depicting miniature buildings, trees, cars, and dry lake beds on land with the other half covered in salt water to represent the sea. It spanned two large airplane hangars. Enclosed in an airtight bubble there was a twenty-foot-wide spotlight at the apex of the ceiling which represented the sun; so bright and hot we had to wear special sunglasses to protect our retinas. On the days I was with him during an experiment I remember sweating like I'd been in a Manduu straitjacket.

The sunlamp's purpose was to create evaporation from the seawater and form a sizable cloud so he could then spray the cloud with known chemicals to enlarge it and then use various combinations of chemicals to draw it to land. I helped him try for two years before he thought he had the right algorithm, which he finally did.

It worked. He was able to seed ocean clouds and coax them over land by using an ingenious principle based on magnetic polarization. We thought the problem was solved. Oceanic cloud seeding would be the answer to save life on earth. And it was, *for a while.*

The drought seemed to be solved. But people ignored the necessary water rationing. Protocols were ignored and more water than ever was being used. Not even ocean cloud seeding could keep up with the new-found miracle of rainwater.

Earth plummeted again into dystopia. Current living conditions right now? Deplorable. Only the rich have access to rainwater. Everybody else drinks filtered black water from the water companies. Poorer countries bought tainted water, causing several deadly diseases. Food was scarce again.

As I read on, *CLOUDS ABOVE* became more and more intense. The struggle between Steve Muller (CEO of the nastiest water company) and Grayson Fields seemed so real that I half-way quit looking for similarities of my grandfather's trials and tribulations and started to just focus on the book's story.

I began to feel like I was reliving 2035. I became Grayson Fields, the real hero. I absorbed her into my being. I was there when they poisoned her. I was there with her at the *TIME*'s Person of the Year Dinner for the richest man on earth, Steve Muller. I was there with her when Muller tried to kill her.

At this moment I'm feeling drawn into some sort of vortex. Right now. This very moment. Remember Robin Williams—in that movie *Jumanji*—where he and his playmate were sucked into the game board and found themselves in a different world? That's how I feel.

Maybe I am in a different world. Or maybe this author is clairvoyant. Or a prophet. Or maybe, just maybe, he's written the key to how we could've avoided the worst disaster that decimated our population from six and a half billion to four billion. We lost two and a half billion people to starvation between 2035 and 2042.

Three billion inhabitants gone. Can you imagine? Forty percent of our population perished in seven years. Every country was ordered by W.H.O. to burn the dead, then create mass graves. In America we demanded markers be placed around the mounds.

We didn't heed the water rationing rules. So, we did it to ourselves. Hunger, starvation, plagues, many people say it's God's judgment. I can't argue with that.

What the author of *CLOUDS ABOVE* didn't realize is he was writing a story that came true. Not every detail, but a lot of it. I was astonished. I kept reading and kept coming across some of the same, or similar, ordeals my grandfather faced.

I thought 'If we'd had this book in 2021, we might not be living in this hell hole right now. Honest truth? It's like we're living in the mid-1800s in an agrarian society with limited resources—water, food, fuel.

Coming to the States from Africa after my grandfather's success in 2036, I remember the lead news stories played out over several weeks, about how he had saved our planet and escaped death at the hands of the big water companies. They had almost gotten control of the algorithm—the key to magnetic polarization.

My grandfather was an international celebrity. I thought he might one day be awarded the Nobel Prize for *both* science and peace as Kennedy had promised. There had been discussion. But there soon came a day when people being people ignored the rules and refused to curtail their water usage. So, the Nobel, not even the lottery, or *any* prize, matters anymore. At this point survival is all we can hope for.

I wonder what would have happened had my grandfather read *CLOUDS ABOVE* in 2021. It might have changed everything.

OVERTONES

Larry Fitzgerald

The attic in my house is where I try to spend the least amount of time. Depending on the season, the room is either too hot or too cold. The stairway that leads here is steep and narrow. And the area itself is in total disarray. So why am I currently sitting in my attic? Because I thought I heard music coming from up here. I was pretty sure of it, but I must have been wrong. There is no music. There are no sounds except an occasional gust of wind confronting the dormer where I am sitting. Unfortunately, I have been here long enough now that I am reminiscing over this room's vast arena of memory stimulants, and they have triggered some deep emotions.

I see scrapbooks, trophies, rarely used kitchen gadgets, Christmas decorations, file cabinets, board games, dishes, wall hangings, and...well, you get the idea. This is stuff that somebody should have thrown away years ago. I see a soccer ball from the championship game of a regional tournament played twenty years ago. There are wall plaques, business souvenirs, service awards, and other reminders of previous employments. These things once held significant meaning to my wife and me, but not anymore. She is gone now, and the kids have no interest in them. Why should they? They are busy filling attics with their things.

So that's it then. I will hire some clean-up folks to dispose of this stuff today! As complex as that may be, it is the right thing to do. But, as I pick up my phone to make that call, my eyes are attracted to a partially exposed black case buried underneath a ping pong table that had served as a stacking platform for the past twenty years. I stretch, pull the case from underneath the table, and sit back down with the case on my lap. I stare at it for a time, wondering how many times I had lugged this thing back and forth between home and school. At least a thousand, I bet. Inside the case would be my old trombone. It had been in the attic for years. I cradle it.

However, I am hesitant to open it for some reason. But finally, I pop open the latches, lift the top, and WOW! THE MOST SURREAL, FANTASTIC, AND UNBELIEVABLE PICTURE EXPLODES IN FRONT OF MY EYES!

In a now brilliantly lighted scene, I am back in my high school auditorium, sitting on stage in front of an audience of hundreds of townspeople who had come to a concert. They were there to hear our band play and witness a contest between two trombonists, a competition conceived by our band director months earlier as a fundraiser. The highlight was determining who was the best "Bone Man" in Eastern Oregon's Grande Ronde Valley.

My competitor was sitting across from me, a gifted young man named Martin. Martin was not only an excellent trombonist but also the best athlete in our school. We were both seniors, soon to graduate from high school. Martin was president of our Senior Class, captain of the football team, and our ace pitcher in baseball. Understandably, Martin was the most popular kid in school. He was also a cinch to win the most coveted award given at the end of each school year, the Best Athlete Award. The only award I had a chance to win was the Band Award. To do that, I would certainly have to win this contest. Otherwise, Martin would garner what I considered the two most essential year-end distinctions. I was determined not to let that happen.

Now I must admit, Martin was a good guy. He never let his accomplishments go to his head. He was always humble and gracious to everyone. I'm ashamed to admit it, but this special touch of Martin's bothered me.

And have I mentioned Martin and I were dating the same girl?

The underlying tensions prompted by the upcoming one-on-one competition had cast an unexpected and eerie quiet throughout the auditorium that evening until Conductor Hagerty walked to center stage and picked up a microphone. Holding the microphone at his side, he patiently waited until he knew every eye in the audience was focused on him.

At last, he said, "Ladies and Gentlemen, the time you all have been waiting for has arrived. We are excited to present tonight two young men who have excelled in their musical proficiencies in the Barrymore High School band for several years, even before high school. And now, tonight, you will have the opportunity to see and hear them display their talents as they perform in this friendly competition we have labeled 'Who Is The Best Bone Man in The Grande Ronde Valley?'"

He then introduced Martin and me and explained the details of the contest and the songs we would be playing. I had chosen a spirited march by John Philip Sousa, "On the Tramp," a fast-moving piece that would demand a lot of action and skilled bone-man-ship. I was nervous but ready to perform first, as decided by a coin toss.

My knees wobbled as I walked to center stage. But as I began to play, I felt my confidence kick in and the tension ease. My body started to sway perfectly with the notes coming from my horn. I could feel it. All those hours of practice were paying great dividends. My body, the horn, and the music were in perfect harmony. It was so sweet. I didn't want it to end. But it did, and the audience responded with resounding applause, several "Bravo"s, and "Oh Yeah"s as well. I walked to the back of the stage and took my seat as First Chair of the trombone section of the Barrymore High School Band. I was a proud man. I had nailed it, big time! I glanced at Martin. He graciously gave me a thumbs-up sign. Darn!!

It was now Martin's turn. As he strode to center stage, he showed no signs of nervousness. The tune he had chosen was "In the Mood," an excellent trombone piece.

Martin started playing softly at first. Then, slowly he began to pick up tempo and volume. Soon, this performer was jiving and romping all over the stage, bending and twisting his tall body into weird shapes and contortions. He even jumped upon an empty chair at one point, blaring his horn so loudly he tested the acoustics of our new auditorium, I'm sure. After performing a two-minute tap dance on the chair, he leaped to the floor and continued playing and grooving until he reached the end of his song. He never missed a beat or hit a sour note. He was terrific, and he ended his performance with a slide on his knees to the front of the stage, thrusting his trombone in the air and screaming, "OH YEAH!"

Martin received a standing ovation as he walked back to rejoin the rest of the band. As he headed our way, my not-so-diplomatic friend Don, a trumpet player, leaned back to me and whispered: "You're toast!"

ෂ

Then slowly, everything in front of me miraculously disappeared. Once again, I am alone in the quietness of my attic. After sitting for several minutes, I lift my trombone out of its case and up to my lips. The notes that ensue are weak and strained, indeed not musical. After trying to play a little of "On the Tramp" with pitiful results, I lower it but stay seated, reliving those many long-ago moments. Martin did win the Best Athlete Award and the Band Award. I felt sorry for myself for a short time but got over it. Deep down, I knew he deserved to win both awards.

Besides, I was the bigger winner by far. I won the girl. OH YEAH!! Toni and I were married for fifty-one years before God called her home. Three kids, five grandkids, Oh Yeah!!

I place my trombone back into its case and push it back under the table.

I know one thing for sure by the time I reach the bottom of the attic stairway. These memories will stay where they are until God takes me home too. Then the kids can deal with them after that.

A VESSEL FULL OF GOOD THINGS

Kristie Koontz

"Ordinary riches can be stolen, real riches cannot. In your soul are infinitely precious things that cannot be taken from you." –Oscar Wilde

Chances are high there's a treasure waiting to be discovered inside your home. Hidden among the reel-to-reel tape player, a bicycle with wooden wheels, cuckoo clocks, and old furniture gathering dust in your storeroom, are valuable items that might be worth thousands, or maybe even millions, — if you can figure out how to recognize them.

In the corner, I found a box with an inch of dust. I opened it to find a book, but just not any ordinary book, one really heavy one. It was an old Bible dated back to 1455. As I leafed through the heavy 11 by 16 inch pages with capital letters printed in red, I thought to myself, "money honey." Its pages consisted of two columns of 42 lines each and the handwriting in the book's front said "This copy of the Gutenberg Bible" which made shivers go up and down my arms. In 1978 a copy sold for 2.2 million, so today it's worth "big money honey."

Who wants to be a millionaire? It would only be a temporary transformation. One that will never really satisfy. Short-term emotionalism with no depth, no root, only short-lived joy. God's concerned with the long term. If only people realized the spirit of a man or woman cannot be satisfied apart from God. We are spiritual beings and He doesn't want us to be apart from him forever. The problems are not riches, but our delight in them, making them the center of our universe other than Him. Where is your energy focused? Where is your heart set? What's in your storehouse?

The basic truth of the Bible is Jesus came to set up his kingdom promised in the Old Testament and fulfilled his mission. But it satisfied the Old Testament hope in a way no one expected. We find in the OT a literal physical kingdom where God as Christ reigns, ruling over Jerusalem and the entire world. We've been expecting his return over two thousand years for the final formation of the kingdom at the "end of the age".

In Matthew 13, Jesus tells us seven parables about His Kingdom and what it will be like. Then at the end He asks his disciples, "Do you understand all these things?"

"Yes," they said, "we do."

In responding favorably, it charged them with bringing forth the treasure of both the Old Testament and what would be the New Testament. Although they answered positively, Jesus knew they understood only in part. Even today, we don't know all the answers but believe he came to rescue his creation from sin and death.

Jesus ends by saying, "Therefore every scribe who has become a disciple of the kingdom of Heaven is like a head of a household, who brings out of his treasure things new and old." (Matthew 13:52). His followers were barely understanding the "new" revelation of Jesus' kingdom and how he fulfills the "old" promises of the OT.

Jesus teaches his disciples that this transformation of life is a continually lifelong process. His followers gradually grasp new things He teaches and connect with the tradition of God's Word they already knew. God keeps on giving "new" truths through His word, equal to a storehouse packed with treasures. However, there are "old" unalterable principles such as God's nature, our nature, and the laws of morality that will stand firm until the end.

I found the great revelation of old things in the first five books of the Bible known as the Torah. However, these books remind me of weird relatives who visit on Thanksgiving. For instance, when I read Exodus, it's hard for me to make it out of the wilderness. And the book of Leviticus is like a priestly technical manual filled with ceremonial laws. Who wants to read a book entitled Numbers, except maybe my husband, who's an engineer? My eyes glaze over as I read through the Minor Prophets because I can't pronounce their names. I admit portions of the Bible are hard and take *prayerful study*, *time*, and *effort*, but are well worth it.

"I'm well aware human life fails miserably at keeping my rules. Don't misunderstand why I have come. I did not come to abolish the Law of Moses or the writings of the prophets. No, I came to accomplish their purpose," Jesus said (Matthew 5:17).

"Ok, so why are you using stories to get your point across? You're losing the crowd," replied his followers.

"I speak to everyone in parables for a couple of reasons. One is to teach you hidden lessons from our past, fulfilling the old truth in Psalm 78:2. The other reason is I'm bringing new light to them for people paying attention. I've revealed myself as the Kingdom of Heaven to everyone. Whenever someone has a ready heart for this, the insights and understandings flow freely. But if there is no readiness, any trace of receptivity soon disappears. (Matthew 13:12 MSG)."

He continues, "But blessed are your eyes, because they see and your ears, because they hear. For truly I say to you that many prophets and righteous men desired to see what you see, and did not see it, and to hear what you hear, and did not hear it. (vv. 16-17)."

I wish all roads led to God, and no Hell existed. There's only one thing wrong with that line of thinking. It's not in line with the Bible. I trust the Lord left his Word so we can understand and love him with our whole mind and heart, and with our whole being (soul), which lives on forever.

"Just as I told Mary after her brother died, I am the resurrection and the life. Anyone who believes in me will live, even after dying." Jesus said.

Oh, how the destroyer doesn't want you reading wisdom literature, which guides you to trust in something outside yourself, who rescues you from sin and separation from God. The accuser patrols the earth to see who he can devour and keep out of the Holy Scriptures. He's hungry for any soul he can consume.

The disciples had a very close relationship with Jesus, and he gives them new roles as the head of his house and wants them to take ownership, develop sound reasoning skills, and imitate him in conduct and character. God's word helps us do the same and stay out of the hands of the destroyer. The bottom line is that humanity needs transformed hearts only the Holy Spirit can provide, and which only Jesus can give.

He fulfills Ezekiel 36: "I will sprinkle clean water on you, and you will be clean. Your filth will be washed away, and you will no longer worship idols. And I will give you a new heart, and I will put a new spirit in you. I will take out your stony, stubborn heart and give you a tender, responsive heart. And I will put my Spirit in you so you will follow my decrees and be careful to obey my regulations (vv. 25-27)."

There are only two religions. One is worshiping humanity and places goodness and salvation in human achievement (good works and being a good person). The other path is worshiping God and placing salvation in the hands of divine intervention. God came to humanity in human form as God the Son and provided eternal life for us. He guides us through God the Spirit. One God in three persons will cleanse our filthy behavior and promote good works.

When we return to Jesus and his teachings in Matthew 13, we see Jesus end his day returning to his hometown of Nazareth. There he continued to teach and do miracles, and I can just imagine the townspeople scratching their head in amazement, knowing him as the carpenter's son, along with his brothers and sisters. I can't imagine ignoring, insulting, and refusing to believe in the God of the universe standing there in plain sight.

And they took offense at Him. But Jesus said to them, "A prophet is not without honor except in his hometown and in his own household." This fulfills the old truth in Deuteronomy 18: "I will raise up a prophet like you (Moses) from among their fellow Israelites. I will put my words in his mouth, and he will tell the people everything I command him. I will deal with anyone who will not listen to the messages the prophet proclaims on my behalf. But any prophet who falsely claims to speak in my name or who speaks in the name of another god must die (vv. 18-19)."

Jesus continues his teaching by saying, "My sheep, listen to my voice; I know them, and they follow me. I give them eternal life, and they will never perish. No one can snatch them away from me, for my Father has given them to me, and he is more powerful than anyone else. No one can snatch them from the Father's hand. The Father and I are one (John 10:27-30)."

Jesus' parables call into question our assumptions about the Kingdom. There will be mixed responses to his message, but I hope you lean in to listen and let his Word penetrate its roots into your soul. Remember, the beginning of understanding starts with repentance, and growth results from small steps. But each small step and each new understanding has a significant impact.

As I hold that family heirloom (Gutenberg Bible) in my hands, I rejoice in all my blessings and all my misfortunes, knowing Christ has walked along with me every step of the way. I don't want to be a rich person and recall how I relished a lifetime of great things with no reference to God. "For what will it profit a man if he gains the entire world and forfeits his soul? Or what will a man give in exchange for his soul (Matthew 16:26)?"

In my household, God's Word is my "big money honey" and my plan is for it to go forth and be passed down to many generations. Can you hear Jesus talking to you? He's asking what's in your storeroom.

God's Word must be so firmly fixed in our minds; it becomes the dominant influence in our thoughts, our attitudes, and our actions. One of the most effective ways of influencing our minds is through memorizing Scripture. David said, "I have hidden Your Word in my heart that I might not sin against you." (Ps. 119:11)

—Jerry Bridges

To Cathi— Thank you for your continued support & friendship! Deborah Sprinkle

THE CASE OF THE CURSED COIN

Deborah Sprinkle

Private Investigator Mackenzie Love covered her ears against the noise. She peered into her mug and grimaced. A layer of fine dust covered everything around her—including the surface of her coffee.

Men stomped on the roof above her. Ladders squeaked and loud thumps sounded. With each stomp and thump, age old dust from the attic filtered down through the second floor to the first along with bits of the ceiling.

But it was the hammering that brought Mackenzie to her knees. She slammed her computer and marched out of her office.

"Sam, tell me again why we agreed to do this?" She eyed her partner as she plopped into a chair next to her desk. How could she stay so calm?

"What?" Samantha Majors pulled earbuds from her ears.

"Where did you get *those*?"

"I've had them a while. Don't you have a pair?"

"No." A tinge of resentment crept into her tone. "What if we get a client? How can you hear the phone ringing?"

"Miss P's on phone duty." Sam gave her a soft smile. "I'm sorry, Mac. Here, use these. I'll get another pair."

Ouch. "No, but thanks. I'm sorry for being a grouch." Mac glanced around. "I'm starving. Want to get some lunch?"

"Sure."

Mac held up a hand. Silence. Somehow, that bothered her more than the incessant noise.

"Miss Love? Mrs. Majors?" The foreman from the roofing company stood in the doorway to Sam's office. "I need to talk to you."

"One of my men punched a hole in your roof while tacking down the underlayment." The man took off his cap and ran a hand through his hair. "We'll fix it. But I need access to your attic."

Mac rose and led the way out of the room. "I'll show you."

"Sorry. It shouldn't take much to repair it."

"That's fine." Mac climbed the stairs to the second story. "The attic access is there." She pointed to a door at the end of the room. "Let us know what else you need."

"Yes, ma'am."

Mac returned to Sam's office. "Now. Ready for lunch?"

❧

"I guess they got the hole fixed." Mac heard the staccato hammering as she pulled the car to the curb in front of their office. "I'm glad. The sooner they finish, the sooner the noise stops."

"I didn't realize how bad it was until we left for lunch." Sam opened her car door. "Poor Miss P will need a break."

"Ladies, glad to see you finally made it back." Miss Prudence Freebody eyed them over the rim of her glasses. "The roof repair turned out to be quite an ordeal."

"What was the problem?"

"Apparently, there used to be a dormer window on the house in that spot." Miss P furrowed her brow. "Its removal caused some problems structurally that had to be taken care of. And, while doing so, they discovered something in the attic rafters. I told the young man to put it on your desk, Mackenzie."

Mackenzie shared a quizzical look with Sam. "Let's see what they found."

A small brown box bound with yellowed tape lay on Mackenzie's laptop.

"May I suggest gloves?" Miss P said.

"Good idea." The three women pulled on clear plastic gloves.

Mac snipped the tape and lifted the lid. A piece of lined paper folded in fours sat atop a wrapped parcel. She spread the paper out on her laptop.

"Beware! Put this back where you found it and forget you ever saw it! G.L."

"That's got to be Uncle George." Mac pointed to the initials at the end. A frown creased her brow as she stared at the small box. What could it hold that was so terrible?

"Are you going to open it? Or shall I?" Miss P leaned closer.

"I'll do it." Mac lifted the tissue wrapped object from the box and placed it on the table.

Round, flat and hard. She relaxed a little. Nothing like a finger or ear or any other gross body part. She unfolded the paper to reveal a dull silver coin.

One side was engraved with an eagle with a snake in its beak and another grasped in its talons, and the other with a strange shape in the middle with spikes radiating from it. What could be so ominous about a simple piece of metal?

"May I?" Miss P examined the coin with her magnifying glass. "There's inscriptions on both sides, but they're too worn to read."

"I'll do an internet search." Sam took photos and stripped off her gloves. "There's something familiar about the eagle."

Mac replaced the coin in its box. "My uncle had a friend who's still in the area. Maybe he'll know something about it." She put the note in a clear sandwich bag and placed both in her top drawer. "I'll go see him tomorrow."

A knock sounded on the back door. Mac answered it.

"I'm sorry, Miss Love, but we'll need to stop for the day." The foreman stared at her roof. "There's not much left to do, but I'm not sure when we'll be able to finish. I'd hoped to be done today. We're scheduled to start another job in the morning." He scratched his chin. "I'll let you know tomorrow."

"Do the best you can." Mac's spirits fell. The new roof was turning into a real headache—in more ways than one.

"Morning, Sam." Mackenzie handed her partner a to-go cup of coffee. "Ready? I'm curious to see what Uncle George's friend has to tell us."

"Me too. I couldn't find anything on the internet." Sam took a sip. "But I know I've seen that design somewhere."

"Hopefully, Mr. Williams is still sharp and can remember something helpful." Mac backed out of the driveway.

Ten minutes later, Mac pulled into a parking space at Leisure Years Care Facility. Inside, Mac and Sam approached the information desk.

"We're here to see Robert Williams." Mac gave the receptionist her best smile.

"Sign in." She indicated the clipboard on the counter. "Are you family?"

"He's an old friend of my uncle."

The woman pursed her lips. "He's in the sunroom down that hall."

The voice of a popular gameshow host led them to a large airy room at the end of the hall. A man sat slumped fast asleep in his wheelchair in front of a large screen TV. Removing the remote from his fingers, Mac clicked the television off.

"Is it lunch all ready?" Mr. Williams blinked awake.

"No, sir," Mac said. "My partner, Samantha Majors, and I are here to see you."

"Are you kidding?" He grinned. "Two good looking dames—I mean young ladies want to see me?"

Mac laughed. "I don't know if you remember me, but my uncle was Charlie Love."

Williams squinted at her. "You're Charlie's scrawny little niece?"

Mac nodded.

"Well, well. How is old Charlie?"

"He passed away about five years ago. Cancer."

"Sorry to hear that." Sadness flitted across Robert Williams face. "Not many of the old gang left."

"That's why I'm here." Mac pulled a chair next to him. "I bought Uncle Charlie's house, and recently, I found something in the attic. I was hoping you could help me figure out what it is."

Mac unwrapped the coin and held it out so Robert could see it. His eyes widened and he rolled his chair back a foot.

"I thought he threw that in the garbage." Robert's voice cracked with fear.

Mac quickly rewrapped it and put it in her purse. "Why are you so afraid, Mr. Williams? What is it about this coin?"

Samantha offered him a bottled water. He took a swig.

"Your uncle won that in a poker game a long time ago. After the game, the scoundrel he won it from told him about the curse." Robert Williams took another drink. "But you know your uncle. He didn't believe in curses. He put that thing in his pocket and left for home."

"What happened?"

"As he was crossing the street, he was hit by a car. He ended up in the hospital for a month. The day he got home, there was a terrible storm and a tree fell on his roof." Robert pointed at Mac's purse. "That's when he decided maybe there was something to the curse business after all. Last I heard, he was going to get rid of it."

"I guess he couldn't bring himself to do it." Mac furrowed her brow. "Do you remember the name of the man he won the coin from in the game?"

Williams nodded. "Henry Adams, a no-good, two-timin'— not a nice guy."

"Is he still around?"

"He used to live in Hermann. That's all I can remember." He raised a hand. "But Miss Love, throw that blasted thing in the trash. Or better yet, throw it in the river."

"I wish I could, Mr. Williams. But for reasons I can't explain, I feel compelled to find where it belongs." She gazed out the window. "Maybe then all this curse business will be over for good."

"God's blessings on you."

"Thank you. And thank you for all your help." Mac stood. "I promise to come visit you again. Without the coin."

"I'd like that."

Mac paused in the foyer. "Did you get all that, Sam?"

"Yes." She waved her small notebook at Mac. "I'm guessing our next step is finding Henry Adams?"

"You bet." Mac continued forward.

At the car, Mac climbed into the driver's seat and started the engine.

"Do you believe in the curse?" Sam said.

"No." Mac shook her head.

"Even after hearing what happened to your uncle?"

"He was at a poker game." Mac snorted. "No doubt he'd had too much to drink and stepped off the curb in front of a car. As for the tree falling on his house, storms bring trees down every day."

"Why are we spending all this time trying to find where it belongs? Why not keep it?"

"I don't know." Mac turned to face her partner. "I feel like this happened for a reason. Don't ask me what, but we cleaned the attic out when we bought the house. Why didn't we find the coin then?"

"You're right." Sam clapped her hands. "Where to next?"

Mac pulled her phone from her purse. "Let's see if Henry Adams is listed in Hermann before we make the trip."

"Good idea."

Mac pressed 411. After giving all the necessary information, she was rewarded with a number. She grinned at Sam as a phone rang somewhere in Hermann, Missouri.

"Hello?" A woman coughed into the receiver.

Mac put her phone on speaker. "Mrs. Adams? I'm Mackenzie Love, and I'm looking for Henry Adams."

"You're about three years too late, deary," the woman said. "Whatcha want him for?"

"My uncle won something off your husband, and I'm trying to find out where it came from."

A terrible hacking sound reverberated through the phone. Mac raised an eyebrow at Sam.

"Give us (gasp) a minute (gasp) pet."

Silence.

"Do you think she's hung up?" Sam said.

Mac shrugged.

"Better now." The woman was back. "If it's about that blasted old coin, don't come anywhere near me with that thing."

Mac and Sam locked eyes over the phone.

"I won't. I just want to know where your husband got it," Mac said.

"He bought it at the pawn shop in Washington. You know. The one on Fifth Street? They said a diver found it in the river near there." A muffled cough sounded. "It was the death of my Henry. Carried it in his pocket, didn't he? And ended up with cancer in his privates."

"I sorry."

"It was his own silly fault. The man at the store told him it was cursed. I told him to get rid of it, but by the time he did, it was too late."

The catch in her voice brought a lump to Mac's throat and tears to Sam's eyes.

"Thank you, Mrs. Adams, and again, I'm sorry for your loss."

"My advice to you, deary, is get rid of that thing as quick as you can."

The curse again, and her third warning to get rid of the coin. Why did she feel so compelled to find out where it belonged?

Mac gazed out the window. "If you want to stop, I can take you back to the office—"

She held up a hand. "I'm with you."

Mac pulled out of the parking lot and turned right. "So far, this whole thing has turned out to be an adventure." Mac's phone sprang to life on the console. "Mackenzie Love."

"Miss Love, I'm sorry. We won't make it back to finish your roof this week. We'll try for early next week, but the weather isn't looking too good."

"Thanks for letting me know." Mac turned to Sam. "Did you hear that?"

Sam's eyes widened. "Look out."

Mac whipped her head around in time to see a pickup barreling through the red light straight for them, horn blaring. She pressed the accelerator and the little sedan leaped forward as if shoved from behind. The two vehicles missed colliding by mere inches.

She pulled to the curb and peeled her hands from the steering wheel. "Thank You, Jesus, for pushing us out of the way."

"Amen," Sam said.

Mac held up a hand. "No curse talk. Remember?"

Sam nodded and cinched her belt a little tighter.

Mac signaled and pulled in behind a van. "If the coin was cursed, we should have been slammed by the truck."

"I thought you said no curse talk." Sam gave her the eye.

"You're right. I think it's time to head back to the office and get Miss P involved."

As they bumped over the curb into the driveway, their neighbor, Mrs. White bustled across the yard.

"I see you have a new roof." She swept her hat from her head. "Forgive me. I've been taking care of my garden."

"Yes," Sam said. "At least mostly. The back still needs to be finished."

"What exciting case are you ladies working on now?" Her green eyes sparkled with interest.

"Nothing much." Mac started for the porch and stopped. Mrs. White worked for the historical society. It was a long shot, but … "Mrs. White, would you take a look at something for us?"

"Certainly."

Mac thought the woman would faint from excitement. She threw a questioning glance at Sam, who nodded. She withdrew the package from her purse and opened the tissue.

Mrs. White gasped and with trembling hands, gently extracted the coin from its paper nest. "A Spanish silver dollar. Do you know where it came from?"

"We believe a diver found it in the river." A quickening filled Mac's spirit.

"Do you have any idea what this means?" Mrs. White raised an awe-struck face to theirs. "This is proof that the Spanish galleon, Santa Josephus, sunk in the river off the banks of Washington."

"That's where I remember the eagle from," Sam said. "We studied the legend in school in St. Louis. It was bringing money to the nuns of the Society of the Sacred Heart in St. Charles, but it never made it."

"Yes." Mrs. White grabbed her arm. "For years, people have searched for proof that this is where it went down, but no one could find a thing." She gazed at the coin. "Until now."

"I think we've found where it belongs." Mac closed Mrs. White's hand around the coin. "At the historical society." A peace flowed through Mac and she knew her quest was over.

Her phone rang. "Mackenzie Love."

"You're not going to believe this, but we've got some time this afternoon and we'd like to come finish your roof."

"Great." Mac grinned at Sam. "We'll be here."

WHISTLES IN THE ATTIC

Steve Bradshaw

"What do you mean you found your son in a suitcase in your attic…?"

The midnight rain came in sheets. The thunder rolled across the midsouth like a galactic bowling alley. They sat on the front porch with a half-empty bottle of Chivas Regal and an inch of scotch in each glass.

"It all started with the gypsy in Blytheville."

"The old lady at the flea market?"

Travis Pucker nodded as he took another sip and savored the aged whisky. "Not because she's of Indo-Aryan ethnicity or speaks Romani, but because she had an aura— a migrant, a nomad from a foreign land."

"A free spirit," Benson said.

"No. Too nice. Something closer to evil, the underworld. Someone unbound by borders and unrestricted by normal things like—"

"—fear and money." He straightened up when another round of lightning strikes lit up the long, wet country road and tin roofs on barns and outbuildings that peppered the countryside.

Benson Medley grew up with Travis in Dallas. After a cowboy childhood and high school football they went to the University of Texas. After college they went their separate ways. Five years later chance brought them back together in Memphis, Tennessee. Dr. Pucker had accepted an orthopedic residency at Campbell Clinic. Mr. Medley, Esquire joined a top law firm specialized in medical malpractice. Travis was okay with anything that got rid of bad medicine.

"I got a strange feeling the day I met her," Travis said. "That twiggy old lady appeared to be fragile and fearless at the same time. I think that's what knocked me off my game. Confusion opened me up to mistakes."

"You mean allowing a witch to get close to your family?"

"And into my attic, if you know what I mean."

Travis poured more scotch and sunk back into his rocker. "I remember it was a beautiful September day in '84. Joanne was five, Melony seven, and Carol nine months pregnant, ready to deliver at any time."

"That alone should have kept you home."

"Yeah. Well, we all needed to get out of the house. A day trip to Byhalia, Mississippi seemed like manageable fun. It was the last day for this traveling carnival and flea market to be in our area. The kids were all in—carny rides, stuffed animals, cotton candy, and cheap costume jewelry at the flea market. Carol wanted to go for different reasons. We were about to have our third child, first Tennessee born. She wanted to find a southern treasure to commemorate the event, or our baby's first Tennessee Christmas."

"Okay. Continue. I'm still wonderin' how all this got into your attic."

"We went to Byhalia, a relatively short trip. Pulled up to fifty acres of bushhogged fields surrounded by giant oak trees. The girls had fun at the carnival, a dozen rides and games. They probably ate a bail of cotton candy. After about an hour they changed gears. They were ready to hunt for cheap flea-market jewelry. Carol was comfortable and ready."

"Great. Okay. Get to the gypsy part," Benson prodded.

"The place looked like someone had rummaged through a hundred attics and dumped it on a field in Byhalia. Towards the end of our browsing we came across the gypsy. She was on the most isolated corner in the back. She sat alone surrounded by scented candles, costume jewelry, tarnished genie-like lamps, piles of old dishes, some carved walking canes, and a lot of porcelain ragdolls. Old clothes and throw rugs hung on a rope. Behind that, an old white van.

"The old lady had on a shabby black dress and long robe with gold trim. She wore a black felt hat with a sagging brim and occult-like pins and buttons all over it. She also wore a veil. It hid most of her face, not her eyes. They were very dark. Empty. Pupils dilated."

"That would be enough for me. I would have left right then, Travis."

"When she spoke, those eyes darted. When quiet, they stopped on Carol's belly—"

"Well, that's creepy."

"No. Creepy is she didn't care I was watchin' her starin' at my wife's belly."

"Why didn't you leave? None of that stuff goin' on in your attic, and with your son, would have happened."

"You know hindsight. It's always—"

"—twenty-twenty. I'm just sayin'."

"I was ready to leave, but Carol asked the gypsy about one of the porcelain dolls, the one the gypsy called her Christmas Clown."

"Never heard of a Christmas Clown? Just the idea of a clown for Christmas gives me the heebie-jeebies."

Travis leaned closer. "I remember exactly what she said, every single word."

"Oh yeah, there's that famous photographic memory that got you through med school."

"She said, 'Dis boy is my Paddy.' Her voice was as scratchy and worn as her trinkets and baubles and rags. Then her dark eyes shot over to me. She said, 'Jes, I say to you doctor boy. Dis Paddy is me boy.' Her veil puffed with every word. 'Paddy boy is bare-dee special Christmas Clown. Paddy boy want brother. You have boy in mama's belly. He brother. Good.'"

"Good Lord. Didn't that scare Carol?"

"No, because the gypsy asked her, 'You want to hold me Paddy boy?' She cradled it like a newborn. I watched Carol's eyes dilate and her smile grow. She was in a trance. I'm pretty sure I was too because I saw that gypsy's sinister smile and could not intervene. I was frozen."

"How'd she know you were having a boy?" Benson asked as he poured. "I remember you guys didn't want to know the sex until delivery. You had both names ready—Sam and Ellen."

"The gypsy knew. We were being managed somehow. Later,

when we walked away, I looked back. That gypsy lifted her veil—not a tooth in her head—and mouthed…Sam!"

"No way!" Benson lit a cigarette with trembling hands.

"I didn't want that clown. Its frizzy, knotted red hair hung from that cracked porcelain clown head barely attached to the dirty cloth body, an over-stuffed bag of sawdust with arms and legs. Only Christmassy thing about it was the outfit, the red felt pants and coat with cotton trim, a cheap black-vinyl belt with a tin buckle, and black, bubble-toed clown boots. It had a crooked smirk painted on its face. No way that clown boy was comin' home with me."

"Sure. Tell me about the attic. We all know clown boy did come home with you." On Benson's last word more lightning strikes lit the night and sent another cacophony of explosions across the rural Tennessee countryside.

"I guess everyone knows I paid $200 for a Christmas Clown I never wanted. Carol had to have it. Somehow that doll made her happy. When we got home that night the girls ran in the house and Carol waited for me. She never does that. She gave me a big hug and kiss and actually sang into the house. I took clown boy straight up to the attic. Put him in a suitcase and tossed it on the Christmas pile. At least I wouldn't have to look at it for three months."

"When did the whistling start?" Benson asked. Then a knock at the window. They waved to the wives on the other side. "Guess we're spending the night, too late and too much scotch. Trip to Midtown in this weather, not good. Great. This gives us more time. Now, go to the parts I don't know, Tee."

"Right. Okay. Well, we had Sam a few weeks after the flea market. That year we put the Christmas Clown under the tree. Every year we did. And every year I put it back in a suitcase in the attic. The whistle started year two; it was a once-a-month thing, an occasional short whistle-like sound. Year three it got louder, longer, more frequent, and was always unpredictable."

"Did you go up there to figure out what was happening?" Benson asked.

"Of course. I'm not that busy. I even got professionals out to the house to figure out what was causing the occasional whistling sound. The roofers and carpenters found nothing. It did not help that the whistles only happen when we are home alone not thinking about it. I was sure we had a crack somewhere. A certain wind would find it…

"Then the spooky stuff started to happen. The Christmas Clown would suddenly appear in Sam's bedroom, standing at the window facing south. Never the window facing west."

"South is Byhalia. Freaky. Carol said you grounded the girls."

"I did. Thought they were messing with me. No other explanation. How else could it get from the attic to Sam's bedroom. Sam was a toddler, and the girls were always pranking. It took a while before I knew they had nothing to do with it."

"When Sam disappeared from his bed one night."

"Correct." Travis lit a cigarette and sipped his scotch. "Scared us to death. We called the police. Whole neighborhood was out looking for him. Police thought he walked in his sleep like other kids his age, probably went outside. Probably curled up under a bush somewhere. After a desperate, unsuccessful hour looking, I came back to Sam's bedroom to think. That's when I saw Paddy standing at the window."

"And you heard the whistle in the attic."

"No. I heard a whimper," Travis breathed. "I kicked that Christmas Clown across Sam's bedroom. Heard a yelp in the attic! I ran up there and followed the moaning to the suitcase I used for Paddy. Found Sam inside."

"God! How in the world—"

"I got him out. He was fine. He was waking up. Police said he walked up there to play and got into the suitcase—like a little bed—and went to sleep."

"No way," Benson puffed.

"I didn't buy it either. I knew then what was really happening. I did not say anything to anybody. I just bagged clown boy and drove to Byhalia that night. This time those fifty acres were empty except for an old white van parked under that gypsy's giant oak tree."

"She was waiting for you?" Benson sank in his rocker with saucer eyes. "I'm sick."

"She said, 'Too much death in attic—dead toys, too many boxes of dead memories. Some broken and others now evil. One time cherished now abandoned and imprisoned in attic. You sent me Paddy boy there. I make you come this night.'"

"What kind of power—"

"I laugh now. I'm over it. We are professionals. There's no such thing as witches."

"You're going there? Are you kidding me?" Benson huffed. "Come on, Travis. You know better. Yes, we are professionals, smart people. And we are smart enough to know no way everything in this world is understood."

"Maybe, maybe not."

They turned to the dark horizon. The lightning was moving south. "No maybe's, Travis."

"In 1984 that gypsy told me Paddy wanted a brother. He went home with us. We tossed him in the attic. When I took him back she said we failed. We put him with our dead memories, forgotten treasures, and rats. She said we did not deserve Paddy. Nothing lasts with us, so maybe now it is our time to be forgotten."

"Whoa. Does Carol know this?"

"No one knows I took it back. Who's gonna believe any of this? My kids have moved on and Carol's not going to poke around the attic for missing memories."

"I think you're dealing with a real witch, Travis."

"Maybe so."

"I hope you dodged a bullet by taking Paddy back. That clown was important to that old woman. If you're lucky, she might have taken your name out of her book."

Benson poured the end of the Chivas. They sat in silence. On that stormy night nobody heard the whistles in the attic except Sam standing asleep at the bottom of the attic stairs…

AUTHOR BIOS

KAY DIBIANCA is a former software developer and IT manager who retired to a life of mystery. She's the award-winning author of the Watch Series of cozy mysteries. Kay and her husband, Frank, live and write in Memphis, TN. Connect with Kay on her website at https://kaydibianca.com.

BETH KREWSON CARTER received her degree from Meredith College, then went to work for Procter & Gamble. Later, while raising a family, she taught school for several years. She studied creative writing with Laura Grabowski-Cotton and has written for *Woman's World* magazine. She currently lives in Tennessee with her husband and the youngest of their three children. *Poison Root* is her second novel, *The Nest Keeper* was her debut in 2019.

BARBARA RAGSDALE is an award-winning writer in short stories. She is published in three Chicken Soup for the Soul anthologies and multiple short-story collections published by CC Writers. Her story "A Walking Miracle" is published in Guideposts' *Miracles Do Happen*. Her poem "Final Moments" will be published in *Cun, Sir! Moments*. She was a columnist and staff writer for *Southern Writers Magazine*. When not writing, she is an exercise instructor with the Silver Sneakers program.

GARY FEARON is a writer, producer and musician. He has written over 300 songs, advertising jingles and morning show parodies. His published works include short stories and the books *After Abbey Road: The Solo Hits of The Beatles* and *Right Brain Writing: Creative Shortcuts for Wordsmiths*. Visit him at www.garyfearon.com.

NANCY ROE has self-published eight books. *The Accident* won the Gold Quill Award, and *Butterfly Premonitions* won First Place for the first chapter. Nancy is a member of Sisters in Crime, The League of Utah Writers, and Newsletter Chair of the Newcomers Club of the Greater Park City Area.

ANNETTE COLE MASTRON started her writing career in the insurance industry working for over 35 years as an investigator, writing reports for a variety of clients. In 2012, she changed careers to work as Communications Director for *Southern Writers Magazine* and its blog, Suite T. She wrote for both the magazine and blog until it closed. A charter member of CCWriters, she is contributing author to twelve anthology books and is writing her first book. She is Editor-in-Chief of this anthology.

RONALD LLOYD: Over the years, I found myself rewriting plots in my head or jotting down an outline on scraps of paper. At sixty-six I retired to a back booth of a Burger King and began writing. Hope you enjoy what I created as much as I have enjoyed writing it.

KAREN BUSLER is a professional symphony orchestra musician (retired), writer, choir director, Bible study leader, and amateur chef. She has been a finalist and third place winner in *Southern Writers Magazine* Short Story competitions. Her full life includes writing, swimming, singing, studying, hosting parties, or making her award-winning chili! Contact her at www.karenbusler.com.

FRANK DiBIANCA devotes his retirement years to writing suspense novels, like *Laser Trap* (A Quincy U Suspense*)*, containing a sauce of romance, mystery, and action on a bed of faith. His employers included the Fermi National Accelerator Laboratory, General Electric Medical Systems, U North Carolina – Chapel Hill, and U Tennessee Health Science Center. Frank was the principal designer of the General Electric 9800 CT Scanner. He and his writer-wife, Kay, assist each other in their manuscript development.

WALLACE M. GRAHAM sharpened his pencil by achieving a master's in criminology. Living in Toone, Tennessee, he develops his craft through experiences at the Collierville Christian Writers Club, the Word Weavers of West Tennessee, and multiple edits of unpublished works through Writer's Digest. Through the writing club, he self-published short stories, annually, as part of an anthology. Other official writings fall into the academic areas of interest.

JUDY CREEKMORE wrote for the *Times-Picayune* for 25 years. She published *Celebrating 200 Years of River Parishes History* in 2008 and has penned two unpublished cozy mysteries. Her short fiction has appeared in various anthologies. She encourages others to write by word and example.

NICK NIXON is a published author, illustrator and audiobook narrator of five Peter English, PI novels and six children's books. He also writes articles and cartoons for various publications. He is currently writing a western and another detective novel. And he does illustrations and audiobook narrations for other authors.

SHARILYNN HUNT traded her medical social work career for speaking, writing, and the ministry of intercession. *Together WE Pray*, building effective prayer teams, and *Grace Overcomes Today*, a 31-day devotional format, exemplify her passion for prayer. Other published inspirational stories can be found in the compilation books of Chicken Soup for the Soul Series, Bethany House, and Guideposts publications. https://www.sharilynnhunt.com

JOHN BURGETTE writes in several styles, including poetry, research, sermons, and short stories. He has studied/worked in a variety of areas, including computer/data science, social sciences, research professor, and lay minister. He applies his interdisciplinary background toward his writing methods, as well as in leading writing workshops (e.g., writing technologies; developmental psychology). Besides contributing to several of the CC Writers' anthologies, his creative writing has appeared in *Southern Writers Magazine* and *Tennessee Magazine.*

DOYNE PHILLIPS is the Co-founder, Charter Member, and past Vice President of Collierville Christian Writers. He has contributed short stories to ten of CCWriters' eleven anthologies. He was also Co-founder and Managing Editor of *Southern Writers Magazine*, where he wrote numerous articles and over 230 blogs for their online site.

JAN WERTZ is enjoying retirement life by turning her imagination loose as a writer, photographer, and traveler. One of her travel addictions is to sign on as a tourist with a storm chasing expert and his tour guides. A DAR, her writing frequently includes her family memoirs.

MICHAEL HICKS THOMPSON has written a variety of short stories along with six novels, winning several major literary awards, including *The Selah* award for Best Mystery Suspense for *The Rector—A Christian Murder Mystery*. Be on the lookout for his latest thriller, CLOUDS ABOVE, a plausible sci-fi suspense novel of a 2035 world without clean water. Available on Amazon. You can see his work on MichaelThompsonAuthor.com.

LARRY FITZGERALD is a retired businessman who enjoys writing Christian fiction, including romance and mystery. He is a former youth soccer coach and feels it is important to encourage Christian worldview thinking in the hearts and minds of our young adults.

KRISTIE KOONTZ - Disciple of Jesus. Wife to Jerry. Mother to Grant and Trent (Trent is with the LORD). Bible study leader. Dog therapy enthusiast. Author of *Pondering Kingdom Parables*. Graphic artist for book covers. Retired Field Sales Rep. Toastmaster. She enjoys working out, walking, talking, golfing and racquetball.

DEBORAH SPRINKLE has written three romantic suspense novels that together make up the series Trouble in Pleasant Valley. She's won many awards, including one for a short story called *Progressive Dinner*, which is the inspiration for her new mystery series set in Washington, Missouri. Connect with Deborah at https://authordeborahsprinkle.com/.

STEVE BRADSHAW, Forensic Investigator, Biotech Entrepreneur, Darrel Award Mystery/Thriller author and Ghostwriter with 10 novels (softcover/eBooks) and 5 audiobooks (Amazon Audible) available worldwide, and 1 screenplay TERMINAL BREACH. Steve is currently writing Book II of The Hillsborough Trilogy for release Fall 2022, and a new novella series John Ritzinger—PI for release in the Spring 2023. www.stevebradshawauthor.com

Made in the USA
Middletown, DE
24 October 2022